For the people who do their Halloween shopping in July, this one is especially for you...

Table of Contents

Table of Contents

Table of Contents

Dear Reader,

Welcome to my pumpkin spice scented guidebook! (*Why aren't scratch & sniff books a thing*?!)

I should probably introduce myself before we dive in. My name is Megan Annie Scott, although my pseudonym is Apple-bobbing Annie. Annie is my middle name and my grandma's name. I love being Apple-bobbing Annie. It makes me feel so quaint and spooky, and close to my grandma, who I never got the chance to meet, as she died before I was born. I got the idea for the name from an art print I ordered online. It depicted a line of monsters waiting to apple bob. Thus, my online Halloween personality was born!

I have loved writing stories ever since I was tiny. For as long as I can remember I wanted to be an author. I was always reading, always checking books out of the library or buying books in WHSmith and Waterstones. I knew the next big thing was to write my own book. Unfortunately, a lot of these dreams began and ended with "Chapter 1 by Megan Annie Scott" to the point that it's become an inside joke in the family. I've filled notebooks with half-finished ideas and character profiles. I would get as far as planning the characters and then the brainstorming train sped off to Timbuktu without me.

In my late teens I could feel the urge to write getting stronger and stronger. I was *desperate* to write something, anything! I wanted it more than life itself. I just had too many ideas brimming over and I couldn't control what direction I went in with them. Around 2022, I decided that I wanted to write an actual book. I had an idea of where I could start. I wrote it all down and mapped out exactly what I was writing in what parts etc. At the beginning of 2023 I began properly writing, and the result (hopefully) is this book! Honestly, I was shocked at every writing milestone. 20 pages, 55 pages, 90 pages etc. I'm still so amazed that I managed to write so much.

A little bit about me; I am a bewitcher of little children (Childcare Practitioner). A witchy librarian and a picnic lover. I live in Newcastle upon Tyne, England, where the lack of Halloween all year around is very sad. There is no Spirit Halloween where I'm from. Pumpkin Spice Lattes only come out on the 1st of September, pumpkins come out of hiding when the leaves turn brown and there is a serious lack of Halloween representation in the media. I follow a lot of Halloween profiles on Instagram; they gave me lots of inspiration to make my life spookier. Most of them were American, however.

It's always been a dream of mine to experience Halloween in America. To step into a Spirit Halloween and see all the huge scary animatronics gazing down at you. To walk through Salem, popping into a shop to make my own witch's broomstick, to travel to Disneyworld Florida and take part in the Oogie Boogie Bash. One day, when I win the lottery! The problem with doing all this though is having to travel to another country. It tends to cost a lot of money! I wanted to do something that I could do on home soil. This is where the story begins...

I decided that I wanted to write my own "seasonal guide", ways of how you can celebrate Halloween 365 days a year. Because I think that Halloween isn't just a day, or a season, but a state of mind. Halloween holds so much nostalgia for me. It reminds me of being little; excited to rush home from school, stand in the kitchen with my Mam as she cut holes out of a bin liner for my costume. As soon as the streets turned dark we were out, knocking on doors, bags held out ready for sweets, acknowledging other kids' costumes. Then it was back home for tea, turning on the telly to watch either *Hocus Pocus* or a Halloween special. It was such a simple time.

Nowadays I have to give props to the online Halloween community. They are the inspiration for this book. The amount of creativity that people have is amazing. They create, sew, bake, recommend, partake in so many different Halloween activities. Also, in the Halloween community was when I discovered holidays such as "Valloween", "Summerween", "Springoween" etc. I didn't realise that you could sprinkle spookiness into other seasons too! That's also an inspiration for this book, indeed there's lots of different inspirations for this book!

Another of my inspirations is the film *Hocus Pocus*. So much so that this book was nearly just a love letter to the film. I could talk about it for hours. Don't worry, there is plenty of love for the film later on! I've loved the film since I was a child, but my hyper-fixation for it resurfaced when I saw that Loungefly was releasing a Hocus Pocus mini backpack. I already had three other backpacks at this point, but once I saw that one, I completely fell in love. At the moment in which I am writing this, I have just received my third HP backpack from a shop called "Be More Geek". It might be my favourite of the trio, but don't tell the others! It's the little things that make you happy.

I always liked the trope "kids fight supernatural forces", now what's more supernatural than three kids teaming up with a talking black cat and a zombie to fight three ancient witches on Halloween night? Throw in some hijinks, peril and a jazzy song and you've got Hocus Pocus! I always remember one scene in particular, when Winifred throws Max up against the wall, and makes him levitate with her powers. The colours stuck in my mind. I was one of those kids who remembered the little details about films. The violet-coloured sky when they were conjuring up chaos, Winnie's burnt orange hair and emerald green robes, the ghostly grey of Binx and Emily when they reunite. Whenever I think of the film, it makes me so melt with joy. I couldn't not be inspired by the Sanderson Sisters.

I'll explain a little bit about how this book works. Think of it like a calendar. We start with December as it's technically the first Winter month of the year. We go through the calendar and finish with November as it's the last Autumn month of the year.

Dear Reader

It feels very poignant to finish with Autumn as we have Halloween in Autumn, and this book is essentially a full circle moment.

There is so much that has gone into this book. History, traditions, crafts, my love of Halloween, my life. I wanted to include parts of my life because as my Granda once said "Write about what you know". That's probably one of the best pieces of writing advice I've ever received. One thing I know, I love Halloween. On that note, I hope you enjoy this book! It's been a long time coming. Happy Halloween!

Love from, Apple-bobbing Annie

Winterween

December to February

Dear Winterween,

The twinkling lights of Creepmas are fading, Krampus has retreated back into his dark and dingy cave for the year. All the Gingerdead men have been demolished. The monster wreaths have been packed away and it's time to restart the sinister clock once

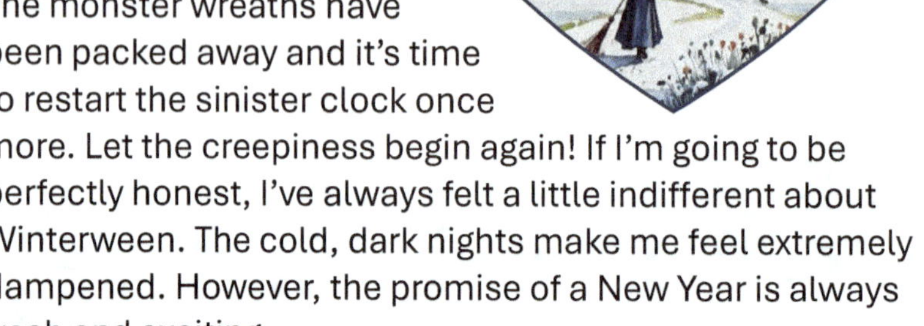

more. Let the creepiness begin again! If I'm going to be perfectly honest, I've always felt a little indifferent about Winterween. The cold, dark nights make me feel extremely dampened. However, the promise of a New Year is always fresh and exciting.

I've realised that January makes me feel tired (from all the oversleeping at Creepmas!). I can barely keep my eyes open most days. With the mixture of tiredness and the damp and drizzly weather, January makes me feel like a zombie. Winterween is the perfect time to embrace feeling like a zombie.

When I was little, I was terrified of zombies. Whenever Michael Jackson's Thriller music video would pop up on the music channels on television I would cry and hide behind a cushion. My Mam would reassure me that he was "just a big cat" when he turned into the werewolf. I wasn't afraid of the wolf. I was afraid of the wide eyes and his gaunt face when he revealed himself as a zombie. It haunted my childhood (not in the good way either!).

In 2021 however I was able to properly conquer my zombie phobia as I watched the film "Shaun of the Dead" for the first time. It became my comfort film. I watched it every single day in January 2022. There was something about Edgar Wright's quick wit, his clever transitions and the characters that completely entranced me. I was quoting the film nearly every day. Slipping little 'Ed-isms' into my everyday conversations.

"Shaun of the Dead" is a big inspiration for the Winterween section of this book. I wanted to include it because it has such a significant impact on me. You don't need to let the cold winds of January dampen your Halloween spirit. I wanted this section to make you feel like you can take on a horde of zombies in London yourself! Be the zombie slayer you were always meant to be!

After January we have February. February is vastly different. Valloween (creepy Valentine's Day) is like biting into a dark chocolate filled with sweet, raspberry goo. Valloween is the love potion brewed by a hypnotising witch, that lives in the Victorian mansion in your small town. Valloween is the pretty pink present you receive, all rustled up with a bow, but when you open the lid, you find a severed toe (with the nail painted red of course, I'm not a monster!).

Valloween is the bittersweet ending to Winterween. With the sugary sweet Valloween it brings the promise of Springoween arriving soon. Lighter nights, warmer days, beautiful sunrises... and so much more spookiness to come! Before we move onto that season though, I want you to get lost in Winterween. It's like being in a snow globe, shake up all the snow (*build a pumpkin snowman while you're at it*!) and then let the snow settle. Enjoy!

Winterween: December

> *"Well, I wish it could be Christmas, every day.*
> *When the kids start singing and the band*
> *begins to play. Oh, I wish it could be*
> *Christmas everyday, let the bells ring out for*
> *Christmas!"*

Wizzard.

Oh boy, I do love Christmas! From this book's premise you would think that I love Halloween, and I do, but the other half of me *really* loves Christmas. When I'm not trying to make everything spooky, I'm gushing over fairy lights, cheeseboards, tacky Christmas jumpers and Christmas films. There's no in-between with me! My most popular Christmas hyper fixations are The Grinch, Nativity (the film, not the primary school play) and Elf. You might also catch me watching Christmas specials of my favourite sitcoms.

- *The Christmas Lunch Incident* (The Vicar of Dibley)
- *The Perfect Christmas* (Miranda)
- *Cold Turkey* (Still Game)
- Every Gavin and Stacey Christmas special!

I will watch these at least 20 times throughout December and sometimes even in November! It really does get you in the holiday spirit. But you're not here for the normal Christmas, you're here for spooky Christmas, or shall I say... **Creepmas!** The holiday that overlooks the bright lights of Christmas, and draws out all the festive spirits from the shadows with their Santa hats...

Luna Alternative Christmas Market (4th December)

Going to a Christmas market is normally a cosy Christmas activity to take part in. Wrap up in a warm outfit, grab your friends and family and have a wander around these quaint little stalls, selling everything from food to gifts and even accessories. A lot of people in the UK tend to head to Edinburgh, because they always have a massive Christmas market, which is more like a mini-Disneyland. However, we have our own Christmas market in Newcastle! I love walking round, it's even prettier at night with all the fairy lights twinkling.

Visiting an alternative Christmas market was something that I never thought I would do. I had seen one advertised at Wylam Brewery; an alternative Christmas market that showcased so many small businesses. My Mam and I decided to take a trip along and see what it was all about. It was like Goth Heaven! There was live music playing, stalls ranging from food and drink, jewellery, pins, badges, spooky accessories, embroidery hoops, candles, wax melts etc., the atmosphere was the best you could imagine. I had to restrain myself to stop from buying from every stall! I really wanted to concentrate on buying Creepmas items so that I could wear them throughout the month.

Creepmas market haul

- I firstly bought two necklaces. One was a candy cane design with a skull ribbon. The second was a "Adopt a Ghost" necklace. A tiny little ghost in a cork-secured jar on a chain. I couldn't resist the ghost holding a candy cane!
- I then pottered over to another stall which was selling kitsch prints and badges. I got a set of three mushroom badges and one pumpkin as well as the stall owner's own designed picture books!
- I bought a "Christmas Mystery Box" from another stall, which has a pin, some prints, stickers and earrings in it.
- Lastly, I couldn't resist an Eddie Munson print and some horror icon stickers!

If you're not a fan of the mundane Christmas markets, I would look into exploring the idea of an alternative market! Even if you don't happen to see anything you like the look of, it's just nice to go out and explore.

Krampusnacht (5th December)

The Grinch is no longer the scariest Christmas character you've heard of! In Germany, on the 5th of December they celebrate "Krampusnacht". The holiday is celebrated the night before "The Feast of St Nicholas" by people dressing up as Krampus and chasing naughty children through the streets! Krampus is a half-goat, half-demon creature who punishes misbehaving children at Christmas. His name is derived from the German word "Krampen" which translates to "claw". I don't think I've ever heard anything so scary but so fun at the same time!

According to legend, he is the son of Hel, the Norse God of the Underworld and originated from the Winter Solstice Pagan ritual. He is essentially the "bad" counterpart to St Nicholas. Where the jolly man with a white beard rewards good children with presents and sweets, this horned monster punishes bad children, by carrying them off in his sack. On Krampus Night, children leave a boot outside of their bedroom door. In the morning, the good children wake up with a present or sweets, the bad children wake up with a "rod" in their boot.

People alternatively celebrate Krampus Night by "Krampuslauf" which translates to "Krampus Run" and involves people dressing as the horned monster, carrying cowbells and sticks (which they use to poke people with) and chasing others through the streets. They also like to get drunk while doing this. I'm not going to lie; this sounds like a typical night out in Newcastle! I've also read in other parts of Europe where they celebrate it such as Austria, they have a huge Krampus parade, where people march the streets, dressed as Krampus, some people doing stunts like acrobatics or fire-breathing etc. It really is the wildest event!

I love that these people have created such a unique holiday that doesn't necessarily highlight the jolly side of Christmas. I feel like the energy at this parade would really be electric. Which looking into the research for this I've come across photos and videos of people in the parade or doing the Krampus Run and it looks terrifying but completely other-worldly. Now, if you can't travel to these places and participate in the actual event, here are some low-key ways that you can celebrate Krampusnacht! Just remember to be well-behaved!

- Study Germanic Lore. Just by researching into the lore and the history of the holiday can really make you feel immersed in the tradition.
- Wear red and black. Subtle but can make you feel very devilish!
- Watch the *Krampus* film. I watched this a few years ago at Christmas and then again on a sick day and I really enjoyed it! It's a creepy comedy that is bound to get you both in a spooky and festive mood!
- Make a Bundle O' Birch Twigs. These can be placed on your doorstep to ward off bad spirits or keep them under your Yule Tree to honour Krampus.

I've found that Krampus isn't the only evil creature who punishes naughty children, or just scares the living daylights out of them, on Christmas. So here are a couple more Christmas creatures you wouldn't like to bump into on a dark and wintery night!

- Mari Lwyd (Wales)
- La Befana (Italy)
- Frau Perchta (Austria and Bavaria)
- Gryla and the Yule Cat (Iceland)

Christmas Jumper Day (8th December)

Who doesn't love a good Christmas jumper? I say, the more garish the better! My Mam and I have a vast collection of Christmas jumpers between the pair of us. She used to work in the supermarket Tesco and every Christmas she would wear the selection of Christmas jumpers in the store throughout December. I would wear them to school, and then during college and now to work when the festive season rolls around.

Nowadays you can get so many styles of Christmas jumper, even themed around films and TV shows. I bought a *Jack*

Skellington jumper a couple years ago, and I also have my favourite *Stranger Things* jumper. If you're a person who enjoys adding spooky pieces to their wardrobe, then you will enjoy wearing a scary jumper for Creepmas! I paired my *Stranger Things* jumper with a checked red shirt underneath and black and red striped tights. It was most definitely a look.

Christmas Card Day (9th December)

> *"That's why I send all my Christmas cards on the 1st of November, gives people 7 weeks to enjoy them!"*
>
> Pam, *Gavin and Stacey.*

I totally agree with Pam in this quote. What is the point of sending Christmas cards during December, when they'll be taken down after a couple of weeks! But I'm a bit of a card hoarder in general. When I was little, I had a yellow plastic trolley decorated with Disney Princess stickers that I kept all of my birthday cards in. I still have most of my birthday cards from when I was 10!

But with Christmas cards a lot of them are only up on mantelpieces or stuck around doors for a few weeks before they're recycled or chucked away. I think that if you're going to make a Christmas card for someone, it should be special. You can get many Christmas cards on places like Etsy where they have Creepmas cards, and a lot of small businesses that are spooky produce Creepmas themed cards for the season. Even if you don't want to buy one you could try and make your own!

Cosy Cinema Day (11th December)

This was such a fun day! Myself, my cousins, and my cousin's friend decided to go to the cinema one day, as a cinema which was local to us was showing a lot of classic Christmas films like *Home Alone*, *The Grinch*, *It's a Wonderful Life* etc. We decided to go and watch *The Nightmare Before Christmas* because it's a collective favourite of ours. I mean, it is the ultimate Creepmas film! So, because I'm extra, I dressed up for the occasion. Not in actual costume of course but I had my *Jack & Sally* t-shirt on and my Santa Jack Loungefly backpack ready for the day!

It was mad seeing the film on the big screen. It had actually been a while since I had even watched it, but as soon as it came on, I felt that excited kid in me start to dance, and I was singing along to the songs silently behind my mask (this was still during Covid times, so we had to wear face masks in the cinema) and feeling all the Creepmas vibes! After the film finished we ended up having a lovely night in my cousin's new flat with a cheeseboard and drinks. It certainly was the cosiest of weekends!

Gingerbread House Day (12th December)

What's better than a Gingerbread House, then a Haunted Gingerbread House?... Decorate your house as you would, whether you're using an actual gingerbread house making kit or making it from scratch. Imagine the gingerbread house from *Hansel and Gretel*, and then add some red icing dripping down from the gingerbread walls, *The Shining* bloody elevator style, around the door etc. Bonus points if you have Halloween sweets left (they shouldn't run out of date too quickly!) you can decorate your house with them e.g. marshmallow ghosts, gummy eyeballs, jelly zombie fingers etc. This is a great activity to do on your own or with friends. Have a competition to see who can make the spookiest gingerbread house! Winner gets to eat it themselves; the loser has to watch *The Shining* in a dark room alone...

National Cocoa Day (13th December)

Cocoa is basically what Americans call "hot chocolate". I love a good hot chocolate and it's one of my favourite hot drinks to have around Christmastime. Plenty of milk, topped with a mountain of squirty cream and dusted with hot chocolate powder plus Christmas sprinkles. I have a few spooky mugs that I can have a Christmas Hot Chocolate in. If you do that then you can have a "movie night" as well!

Around August, YouTubers Zoe and Mark had a "Halloween-Christmas night in" where they decorated the sitting room for Christmas, wore a Halloween t-shirt with Christmas pyjama pants, watching both Halloween and Christmas films and eating a cheeseboard with other snacks. It's one of my favourite videos of theirs, so much so that I recreated it in either 2020 or 2021. Wearing my Christmas *Wham* t-shirt and *Stranger Things* pyjama pants, making a hot chocolate in my gingerbread man mug, watching *The Holiday* and a cartoon Halloween special on Netflix. It was such a cosy night!

Go Carolling Day (20th December)

Carolling is something that isn't necessarily a British tradition. Although there's places that do it in the UK, it's more of an American tradition. In fact, in the beginning of *The Addams Family* film, you've got a lovely clip of a group of carollers, dressed in authentic historical costume singing at the Addams Family's front door, before it pans up to them creeping on the roof, ready to pour a vat of steaming hot liquid onto them before it flashes to a title card!

Carolling is the tradition of going door to door (a bit like trick or treating…) and singing traditional Christmas Carols. Sometimes people do it for charity, other times it's just for the fun of it! There are so many Christmas carols, and not enough Creepmas carols! If you're brave enough, you could go around your local area, with some other people and sing Halloween songs as carols! Songs such as *The Monster Mash, Flying Purple People Eater, Incy Wincy Spider, I Put a Spell on You* etc. If you do it in costume it will be even better!

Ghostly Christmas Eve (24th December)
Haunting History

It's finally Christmas Eve; it might even be better than Christmas Day (controversial). The Victorians had a spooky tradition to tell ghost stories around the fireplace on Christmas Eve. Many people finished work early on Christmas Eve and would retreat to warm homes with a roaring fireplace and candlelight. Telling stories seemed like a natural way to pass the time. The release of *A Christmas Carol* in 1843 only heightened this belief of ghost stories, with Scrooge being haunted by three Christmas ghosts. The rise of ghost stories being printed was becoming more popular, but families still wanted that traditional story-telling vibe, to bring the family together. The link between the paranormal and Christmas dates back hundreds of years, to the spiritual Winter Solstice celebration.

I agree that there's definitely an eerie feel to Christmas that people might overlook. It helps when there's supernatural stories, legends, and folklore of creatures like Krampus or the Yule Cat to spook you on a cold, dark night. It wasn't just parents telling their children these stories to scare them into behaving and eating their vegetables, but stories to keep you entertained on a night where the snow won't stop falling outside your window. So that's what Victorians did. On Christmas Eve, they would gather around a warm, crackling fireplace with their family, sharing ghostly tales over a mince pie. It's a tradition that we need to bring back, so if you have a spare candle going, tell a ghost story instead of watching *The Grinch* this Christmas Eve!

Winterween: January

Happy New Year! After all that overindulging of food and drink and watching Christmas films, paying the occasional sacrifice to Krampus, it's time for a fresh New Year! Some people find new year to be exciting, 365 days of new ideas and promises laid out in front of you. Others (like me) can find it quite daunting and overwhelming. The idea to be perfect and on top of my game can be a struggle. Just remember, life is what you make it, don't let other people's ideas of perfection get you down. Make your year what you make it and don't let anyone tell you how to live your life!

I also suffer with "post-Crimbo tiredness", the kind of tired where you wake up tired? Yes, that's me. I slump around in pyjamas when I'm not at work, struggling to keep my eyes open, occasionally grunting at people if they ask me a question. I feel like a complete zombie. I may as well just start eating brains because I clearly don't have one. The lights are on, but nobody's home. If they are, they're standing by the fridge, finishing off the leftover cheese from Christmas.

In 2023 I decided to embody a different Halloween creature each month. Mostly for my reading, but in general too. Not in a literal sense though. I'm not running around *actually* eating people's brains or casually howling at the moon at night whenever I feel like it. Or casting hexes on my exes, brewing potions, you get the idea! It was more on an aesthetic kind of mission. To live my best spooky life. And what with my obsession with *Shaun of the Dead* in January 2022, can you guess what this month's creature embodiment would be? I'll give you a clue: **braaaiiiins...** You guessed it! A Chupacabra! Only joking. It is in fact a zombie.

National Bloody Mary Day (1ˢᵗ January)

*"We'll have a Bloody Mary first thing in the morning, bite out of the King's Head, couple at the Little Princess, stagger back here and *bang* back at the bar for shots!"*

Ed, Shaun of the Dead.

Now, I'm not a massive drinker. In fact, I have never had a Bloody Mary before! But I thought it would be the perfect opportunity to celebrate, *Shaun of the Dead*-style! If you love pub crawls, then this activity will be for you. What a way to start off the New Year!

Shaun of the Dead: Pub Crawl

I know pub crawls are the main premise of *The World's End*, the third film in the Cornetto Trilogy, but I thought it would fit in well with this activity. We all know and love *The Winchester*; the pub featured in Shaun of the Dead. It's their local that they lay all their trust in to protect them from the zombie apocalypse. And do you know why? It has heavy doors, clear exits, there's a shotgun above the bar, and Ed knows he can smoke in there. How's that for a slice of fried gold?

Step One: Assemble your group together (close friends will do) to take on a horde of zombies in London. Or a round of shots in your favourite pub! If you want, you could dress as the characters from the film because everyone loves fancy dress, do they not?

Step Two: Choose your location. Make sure the whole group agrees on where you want to travel to. Maybe each person could choose a bar or pub so that it's a fair game.

Step Three: Let the chaos ensue! First game of the night is the "You've Got Red on You" challenge. Get some red sticker sheets (little ones will do, the less obvious the better) and hand them out to your teammates. The aim of the game is to stick as many red stickers as possible on random people, without them noticing. If anyone notices, you lose and must have a cocktail of your friend's choice.

Step Four: One of your friends must be the "Pete" of the group. Sort of like an anonymous saboteur, their mission is to find as many ways as possible to "cock up" the night, without anyone finding out they are 'the Pete'. If they are found out (only if the pub you're in has karaoke) they have to sing "Don't Stop Me Now" by Queen.

Step Five: You have to describe the ice-cream "Cornetto" to your friends, without saying the word. If your friend unintentionally says the word Cornetto then they must go on a timed Cornetto hunt e.g., go to a local shop and find a Cornetto in under 5 minutes.

Step Six: To finish the night, everyone has to write down a 'truth or dare' and place it in a pint glass. In turns take out a slip of paper and complete either the truth or dare on it. On your way out of the pub, make sure your last drink of the night is - a Bloody Mary!

Bookish pub date (Ed not included)

You can do this solo, with a friend, a significant other or a family member. It's entirely up to you! With anyone who is willing to read with you. Choose your Winchester of choice. Whether that's a local pub, a cosy pub that's took your fancy, or a pub with a haunting history. Make sure you know where the exits are, bring your weapon of choice (a zombie book would suffice!) as well as your Ed/Liz.

Grab a pint from John and then choose a table (avoid sitting next to Snake Hips!) and begin to read! Get swept up in the atmosphere of the background bar conversations and light music. Hopefully it isn't a busy night when you go, so you can enjoy your book in peace, exchanging mini reviews with your date. Follow along the story and soak it all up with a pint! Some zombie books I'd like to recommend are:

- Alice in Zombieland
- Wranglestone
- Timberdark
- You've Got Red on You
- Dawn of the Dead

Shaun Sleepover & Eyeball Hot Chocolate

This one is fairly easy but have a sleepover or a chill movie night on your own and make a hot chocolate, layer it up with swirls of squirted cream and pop some eyeballs in it! Not actual eyeballs of course. Usually at Halloween they do chocolate eyeballs, or even gummy eyeball sweets, if you have any left from Halloween, I would use them to decorate my hot chocolate.

And the main event is of course, watch Shaun of the Dead. If you want, you could also watch other zombie films or TV shows (I started watching *All of Us Are Dead* in 2022) during the night. Try not to get nightmares! If you want, you could even create a trivia quiz to do while you're watching Shaun, to see how well you and your friends know the film. You might be surprised by how well you do, or how much you don't know about it! Either way, enjoy a cosy night watching zombies chew people up and nom on their brains. How wholesome!

Gary King's birthday (3rd January)

Perfectly coinciding with our New Year events, I found out that on the 3rd of January, it is the fictional character Gary King's birthday! Simon Pegg posted it on his Instagram, and I'm surprised I didn't know that, considering *The World's End* is my second favourite of the trilogy. Gary is definitely the most outlandish character Simon Pegg has played in the trilogy. He's wacky, immoral, goes by his own rules which does come back and bite him in the bum!

Winterland at Seven Stories (7th January)

Going off topic about zombies, but still Winterween themed, we took a trip into a far-off land of snow and ice. My sister found out that Seven Stories (a learning centre for children's books) had an exhibition happening called "Winterland" starting from December until the end of January. There was also a Julia Donaldson craft session happening, and since my niece was obsessed with *The Gruffalo*, we thought we should go and have a look!

On the Level 5 gallery was Winterland. It was a big open-plan room which was decorated to look like a winter wonderland! The floor was dusted with "snow", fairy lights were hung around the walls and fake winter trees were dotted around. There were cosy reading nooks with Christmas and winter-themed books to read, a post-box and Santa's sleigh for the kids to play on. You could take part in a "Scavenger Hunt", a piece of paper you could ask for at reception, ticking off different things within Winterland.

There were also secret side rooms within the gallery, each room themed around a different wintery book, with interactive toys and props. Some of these books included Harry Potter, Narnia, His Dark Materials etc. The rooms that made me feel like a Yule Witch were the rooms which had these books: The Worst Witch, The Wizards of Once, Witch Child, The Witches etc. I loved these rooms especially! One of them had a fake fire, so I could pretend to cast spells into open flames.

'Potions and Herbs' was another part of the side rooms. They had glass jars with magical property spells written next to them, knitted mushrooms, and in the Harry Potter room there was a coat rail of Hogwarts uniforms! My niece was more interested in the toys (they had a basket of forest animal puppets) but I loved reading all the book quotes on the boards. It really felt like I was crunching through thick snow, breathing in icy cold air!

I had the best time pretending to be a Yule Witch, reliving all the wintery books that I read as a child. Afterwards we headed to the craft session, and my niece made two adorable Julia Donaldson character spoons! It was a lovely day out, one that I will always associate with Winterween in the best way.

National Bubble Bath Day (8th January)

January can be a hard month, for a lot of people. If you suffer from seasonal depression, it can feel so dark and lonely. For the longest time, I resented January and New Year's. On New Year's Day 2020, my Granda passed away. He had been in hospital over the Christmas holidays after his dementia had gotten worse. It wasn't a shock that this happened. He was in his 90s and had had a long and adventurous life. However, it was hard for me; he was the first close family death that I had ever experienced. It took me a while to cope. We also had his funeral in January, on the 24th. January carried so much sadness I ended up just spending the month feeling sad and depressed. It took nearly 3 years for me to not feel as sad in January as I used to. My Granda's death still affects me every day. In fact, one of the things that upset me about writing this book is that he won't ever get to read it. He always used to call me the "next Catherine Cookson". But now I know I can still make him proud, even if he isn't here physically.

If you have experienced something similar to me, and resent January, here are some "self-scare" tips for you, to feel more relaxed and happier:

- Make plans in a fresh diary. Whether you have some events that you have organized already; early Halloween plans, reading plans, musicals you have booked etc, just writing them down can make you feel hopeful for the year ahead.
- Mate date with a friend. Give a friend a call and make plans with them. Whether this is a quick coffee date, or a trip to the January sales, it can make you feel better socialising with friends.
- Go for a brisk winter walk. The weather will more than likely be cold and miserable. It mostly is in the UK, but particularly in January. Wrap up in a coat and scarf and go for a walk in your favourite outdoor area. You could tick off things in your head that you see e.g., a robin,

mushrooms, icicles etc. Feeling cold air in my lungs and a fresh breeze on my face always makes me feel refreshed.

- Watch your favourite film. This one is obvious, but watching your favourite film can give you a massive serotonin boost. No guesses as to what film I'll be watching!
- Change your bedding. It's time to change that Christmas bedding and put a fresh set of sheets on your bed! Being in a fresh bed can make you feel so clean.
- Have a bubble bath. Here's the Bubble Bath part of this day! Sit back in a pile of fluffy bubbles and let your troubles melt away. For the perfect bubble bath concoction, I would use Lush's Frozen bubble bar for minty bubbles and "Screamo" (this came in a bubble wand also) bath bomb for the icy blue bath of your daymares! Add your favourite hot drink on the side for extra relaxation.

Winterween Readathon (3rd -9th January)

During January 2022 I participated in a "Winterween readathon" similar to the Summerween readathon that I joined in with the previous year. It's run by the same two Youtubers (Gabby and Olivia) and takes place over the period of a week, with a set of spooky prompts to assign your reads to. I love taking part in seasonal readathons. It's such a cosy week of reading, snacks and hot drinks.

The books and prompts I chose for the readathon were Wranglestone and The Wolf Princess, also starting The Winter Garden which ticked off the prompts "Snow on the cover, Winter Setting, Thrills and Chills". I had a lovely week of reading, I had just received a grey snuddie for Christmas, which was the most *perfect* reading outfit, it was so soft!

I'm surprised I managed to read three and a half books, considering I also went back to work in January after the

Christmas holidays. One day during the readathon I had an early finish from work, so I went home, ran a bubble bath and had a cup of tea in my gingerbread glass mug and started my third book. It really was the most blissful afternoon! My sister also made some brie, cranberry and spinach pastries for us to taste test, so I got to have a delicious snack to accompany my reading! This year (2023) they didn't hold the Winterween readathon in January, so hopefully it'll happen again in 2024!

Winterween: February: (Valloween)

"Love is a magical thing. Love will make you feel like a queen or a king. Unicorns, rainbows, lucky charms. Await you in your true love's arms."

Anna Biller "Love is Magical Thing" (The Love Witch)

Love Witch Spell

Picture the scene. It's Valloween night. You've just finished brewing the sweetest of love potions in your dimly lit Victorian kitchen. The smell of cherries, milk chocolate, pink blossom and strawberries waft through the air as you secure the lid tightly. You begin to climb the stairs, heading to your bathroom to run a bubble bath and indulge in the practice known as "self-care". You browse through your extensive bath bomb collection in hopes of finding the perfect one. Which scent, which colour, which shape to choose? As you begin to run your bath you decide to write a spell, a new spell...

Ingredients for the perfect pamper night:

Bubble Bath Potion:

To create the perfect potion for your bubble bath I would recommend using these products. For the bubbles I used two crystal bath fizzers from Primark's "normie" version of Valloween (known as Valentine's Day apparently!). These both have such a gorgeous, sweet smell to them, and they also turn the bath water a blush pink colour! I also used a sprinkling from my tube of *Hocus Pocus* crystallised bath salts. It gave the water a touch of lavender, heavenly! Crystal bath bombs are the most obvious choice for a witch looking to do some serious relaxing!

Skin cleansing:

To make my skin glow brighter than the moon I used a Raspberry and Pink Lychee body scrub, a whipped Watermelon shower foam and an adorable little pink soap called "Me Time" which was also watermelon scented. All the products were from Primark. I normally go for bath products from Lush, especially bath bombs, but Primark have been pulling it out of the park recently with their bath range. The products are also very affordable so it's hard not to resist! Witches must budget too! I also decided to do a face mask to give my skin some tender loving care! I went with a simple Pink Guava peel-off mask for my face. It was a cheap one I picked up from Superdrug and it honestly made my skin feel very fresh.

Music for the ears:

Music in the bath is either a yes or a no for me. For this occasion, I really wanted to feel the vibes with mystical music in the air. I started off by listening to a few songs by Fleetwood Mac. Stevie Nicks is the most powerful witch in the music industry. That woman does not write a bad song! The song "Rhiannon" makes me feel so relaxed. Since it is written about a witch it is the perfect song to listen to. I also listened to a "Valloween playlist" on Spotify, compiled together by *Spooky Little Halloween*. It had a range of spooky romantic songs, and songs about powerful witches that made *me* feel like a powerful witch!

Film Viewing:

You can watch any witchy romantic film of your choice. The film "The Love Witch" is a retro homage to witch films of the 60s and 70s. Unfortunately, I could not find an available streaming service to watch it on. Instead, I headed to Netflix and chose to watch the 90s film "The Craft". This is about a teenage girl who gets pulled into an unpopular group of girls. Specifically, their coven. As the magic gets to the girls' heads, will it end in the apocalypse? I loved seeing Skeet Ulrich and Neve Campbell in another dark film together. It feels like a more twisted version of "Sabrina the Teenage Witch" for sure! Witch's covens are something that I've always wanted to be a part of a magical circle of individuals. Although, if you read my book, you can be part of my coven!

Warning: if the ingredients in this spell are not carried out correctly, you will not have the greatest mystical experience!

Ghoulish Gift Guide:

One of my favourite things about Halloween is looking for different creepy pieces to go in my collection. I love collecting pins, stickers, prints and bookmarks. The way I do it is to look at small shops. Supporting small shops is a great thing, supporting _spooky small shops_ is even better! I wanted to make this a recurring segment through the book, showing my recommendations and my different picks for different pieces. You can either get these for yourself, for a friend, family member or significant other! In this section I will of course be showing my Valloween gift guide, and all the chilling pieces I purchased from various small shops.

- Scream bookmark (from _ABookishBoutiques_) I have an unhealthy obsession with bookmarks, and I love to theme them with whatever I am reading. I see Ghostface included a lot in Valloween designs so I thought I'd pick up this pink Scream bookmark. It has

Randy's iconic rules written on it, so you don't forget. EVERYONE'S A SUSPECT!!!

- Valloween coffin bookmark (from *WitchatOneandSeventy*) Another bookmark, are we even surprised? I loved the coffin shape of this one. It also has a bit of a naughty message on it if you're into that sort of thing! Cheeky, but it's still a good design! I also didn't realise that the back of the bookmark is velvet. Very soft to slip into your book!
- Dark chocolate box print (from *Simonsnest*) I love a good print! Postcard prints are perfect to collect, especially because they fit into a mini photo frame and pop anywhere! This design is sweet with the creepy chocolate box because who doesn't want skull shaped chocolate?
- Valloween pins (from *SpookySupply* and *BlushBoulevardCo*) I haven't talked about my pin collection yet. It's large. I like to collect a lot of different styles and designs of enamel pins but in particular, Halloween pins are my favourite. I went with the ghost theme again but dotted with little pink hearts. The other pin is ghastlier, with the grinning pumpkin head skeleton holding a huge red heart. They're great to pin on a jacket or even a tote bag!
- All the items in this section were purchased on Etsy UK.

A date with M3GAN.

Celebrating Ghoulentine's Day is a particularly fun part of Valloween. Galentine's Day is the celebration of female friendship, so celebrating Ghoulentine's Day, by doing spooky things with your gal pals is even better! Living in the UK it can sometimes be difficult to do Halloween-related things not on Halloween (hence why I'm writing this book!). But sometimes, activities can be thrown your way without even realising it. Which brings us to having a date with a sassy, murderous AI: introducing M3GAN.

I first heard about the film "M3GAN" in 2022. Just from the name I was excited for it - I'd never heard of a horror that had my name! It made me tremendously happy! As more trailers and advertisements started popping up closer to the film's release the more excited, I got and the hype around the film was getting more popular.

For this Valloween activity I thought it would be fun to go on a cinema date with your friends to see this film! I would recommend wearing your best Valloween outfit with spooky jewellery, pick up some Valentine's themed snacks for the cinema (may not be spooky but supermarkets always release themed snacks around days like these, or you could go with a pink and red snacks theme!).

After the film you and your friends can go for food. Anywhere you like! My personal favourites for food places (in Newcastle) are Nando's (overrated I know, but nothing compares to Nando's mashed potato!), Chiquito's and Smashburger. You can choose anywhere you like for your chosen food place. Going for cocktails is also an excellent choice. You can do that before or after you go for food. If you know a place that does great food *and* great cocktails that's even better! **(Please drink responsibly).**

> *"Think that you can play with me, you better watch your back. The last thing you'll hear is my laugh. Cause' Baby dolls kill, don't provoke us, or we will, push you downhill."*

Bella Poarch.

Monster Romance...

Every so often, us Halloween lovers are blessed with creepy films being released throughout the year, different to horror films in October. It doesn't happen too often, but sometimes we are treated to a "monster romance", which is the perfect film to watch in the cinema on a romantic date for Valloween!

"Monster Romance" is a genre that spans decades, all the way back to the black and white *Universal Monsters* era in the 1930s-1950s. Involving terrifying creatures and humans falling in love. It's a decades old trope that is still going today. Whether that's with sparkly vampires, scaly fish men or teenage zombies... Here are some recommendations that you might like!

- The Bride of Frankenstein (1935)
- Lisa Frankenstein (2024)
- The Brides of Dracula (1960)
- Twilight (2008)
- Warm Bodies (2013)
- Revenge of the Creature (1955)
- The Shape of Water (2017)
- Edward Scissorhands (1990)

My review of M3GAN:

Because I'm a trial and tester I had to watch M3GAN myself. I genuinely enjoyed this film. It didn't take itself too seriously. I could tell the film was very character-driven as opposed to being driven by the gore and the horror. Most of the kills happened in the second act of the film, so the first act was there to develop the character's relationships with each other.

It was surprisingly heart-warming in the beginning! I enjoyed watching the auntie-niece relationship between Gemma and Katie evolve as they're both thrown into an uncertain situation. I could see both perspectives of how they were struggling to deal with this new arrangement. My favourite scene was when Katie and Gemma were discussing all of the toys that Gemma was designing, and she introduced her to Bruce, her original model. Talking with Katie gave her the idea of creating M3GAN in the first place.

The whole topic of doll-like AI machines is something that they seem to be exploring in horror nowadays. It reminds me of when they remade Chucky a few years ago, but because of the subject of technological advancement, Chucky was now a fractured AI doll as opposed to a doll possessed by a demon spirit. It's a commentary on how far humans and technology have come, and I don't see it as a problem.

We then finally meet M3GAN (Model 3 Generative Android), a child-size version of my childhood Bratz dolls that I loved so much. I love the fact that she is so human-like but still has the doll qualities. Her voice is something that I noticed in particular. In the first act of the film, it has that little girl voice with tone of a robot to let us know that the doll is still an AI. However, as the film goes on her voice gets more and more humanoid. This also goes with M3GAN's personality. Her humanoid voice with the sassy lines that she starts dropping really cracks me up.

I enjoyed watching behind the scenes of the film. M3GAN is not completely CGI as I thought she was. She's played by a little girl who is a professional dancer! She wears silicone hands and a mask, and the mask is obviously CGI animated with M3GAN's many facial expressions. M3GAN's voice is played by another girl who did an absolutely amazing job, even when she speaks in real life she still sounds like her scary counterpart. I thought it was really interesting and added extra layers to the film.

The one thing that I loved about this film is that it didn't take itself too seriously. It was goofy in parts (M3GAN randomly decides to sing Katie to sleep), M3GAN does a "TikTok dance" before she decides to hack someone to death, she drives away in someone's car etc. It does seem quite ridiculous but overall, it just made me laugh. If you're in the mood for a scary film that still makes you giggle, I would highly recommend M3GAN, you'll have a killer time!

Witch's Fingers...

"I put a spell on you, and now you're mine. You can't stop the things I do. I ain't lying. It's been 300 years. Right down to the day, now the witch is back! And there's hell to pay."

Nina Simone/Winifred Sanderson.

No, I'm not talking about those luminous green plastic witch's fingers with the long pointy nails that were part of every 90s kids Halloween costumes (let's bring back the binbag witches!). No, not that. I'm talking about getting your nails done for Valloween of course! I personally love getting my nails done. It makes me feel fresh and "swanky posh", as my Grandad's late girlfriend used to say!

My sister, Kayleigh is a mobile nail technician who owns a nail art page called "Pretty Weird Nails" with her friend Nikki. My sister also just happens to be a Halloween enthusiast like me. She has an Instagram page called "PinkTeaVanity" which features all things nail and beauty related. Every Halloween she does "Kayleighween" where she makes tutorials on different SFX Halloween looks. I do love following along every week to see what she comes up with!

I knew I had to get my Valloween nails done by her! My cousin also just happened to have a nail appointment with her, so we decided to make a day of it! One Saturday she drove us over to my sister's house where we got our nails done by Kayleigh. Getting your nails done is always such a therapeutic experience. She even gave me a proper hand wash, my hands felt very soft afterwards!

I ended up going with gorgeous Barbie pink with five little ghosts flying across my nails and sparkly red hearts dotted across. I loved them! After we got our nails done, we decided to go out for lunch afterwards. We ended up in a lovely little farm tea shop, where I had actually been a few months earlier pumpkin picking! We had paninis and coleslaw and shared a bowl of potato wedges. It was nice to spend time with my cousin. We're the same age; I'm a couple of months older than her, so we've always been close growing up. With adulthood getting in the way it can be hard to just sit and catch up, so it well needed! It's also a great Valloween activity idea: getting your talons done and having afternoon tea!

Haunting History

In addition to being a Halloween lover, I also love history. *Horrible Histories* was one of my favourite TV shows when I was a child. I loved learning about different historical traditions, facts and of course the songs were better than anything on the radio! Within this book I wanted to include a lot of history and varied spooky traditions. There will be a focus on local history, as I am from Newcastle, in the North East of England, which is rife with sinister history, though included will be history from all over the world.

Vinegar Valentine's

On the 14[th of] February you might expect to get a Valentine's card pushed through your door or passed a card over breakfast by your significant other. In the 1800s however, Valentine's card could be a little bit different... Between the 1830s and the 1840s, little postcards started to pop up. They were dubbed as "comic valentine's". They were typically a postcard with a caricature drawing and a poem. The poems were mean-spirited, mocking but sometimes were more gentle jabs. You could send them to anyone! An annoying neighbour, a hideous co-worker, a cheating spouse etc. Here's an example of a Vinegar Valentine's that particularly made me chuckle:

> *"To My Valentine / 'Tis a lemon that I hand you*
> *and bid you now 'skidoo,' Because I love*
> *another—there is no chance for you,"*

Nowadays, we would call that a "burn"! In fact, some postal workers would sometimes actually confiscate Vinegar Valentine's if they thought they were too "vulgar". One Vinegar Valentine's even led to a man *shooting* his estranged wife in 1885 because he received a brutal postcard. Ouch! The Victorians were a wild bunch!

Some of these Valentine's were also career targeted, nicknaming physicians as "Doctor Sure-Death" and naming *any* woman an "Old Maid" when they got the chance. An absolute slap in the face! Suffragettes were also unfortunately targeted, diminishing their fight for the vote.

> *"To a Suffragette Valentine, your vote from me you will not get. I don't want a preaching suffragette."*

I don't think you can get any harsher than that! Nowadays, that would be called "shade". However, suffragettes did have their own hand at pro-women's rights Valentine's! One of their phrases that was coined was "no vote, no kiss", which I applaud for being so shady. Many of these savage cards were illustrated by Charles Howard in the late 19th century. As the years went on the strange custom began to get less popular, as the last we heard of them was in some locations in the 1970s.

These Valentine's reminds me of the Valloween cards that I've seen on the internet. A lot of them that I've seen feature popular horror film characters with a romantic line that might not be so romantic...

Some of my favourite examples include:

- Michael Myers: "Let me get all up in them guts" (pumpkin guts)
- Ghostface "Can I *call you,* my Valentine?"
- M3GAN "We make a lovely pair!"
- Jason Voorhees "You make me one Happy Camper!"

The list goes on! If you search them on Etsy, so many different designs pop up for you to look at. I suppose you could say they are the modern Vinegar Valentine's for the spooky generation. Just not laced with vinegar, that belongs on fish and chips!

Love lanterns

In medieval times, a lot of people held banquets to celebrate love. Like going anywhere on Valentine's Day nowadays and seeing lots of people having romantic dates in restaurants. A rather strange food custom that some women would do would be to mash up leeks and earthworms to eat to help strengthen a failing relationship. I wonder if it ever worked. They might think I'm weird, but I'd prefer to just have cheese in my mash, rather than earthworms.

During these banquets, the guests would wear infinity signs and love symbols on their clothes (I talked about buying Valloween enamel pins!) and talk about love over dishes that would "stimulate affection". This is all very interesting but the piece of information I found particularly eerie was that these banquets would be lit by what Tom Hodgkinson described as "Love lanterns" which were essentially hollowed out large turnips. Talk about the ultimate romantic mood lighting! These are obviously very similar to "jack-o-lanterns" which were coined by Irish folk, brought over to America and turned into the beloved pumpkins that everyone knows nowadays. I love that jack-o-lanterns have come such a long way, that they were even used as lighting for a romantic date.

Midnight Rendezvous?

Another tradition that many women tried to do to see their future husband was to head to the local cemetery the night before Valentine's Day. At midnight, they would run around the church twelve times. If you did it properly, you would see your future lover as a ghost, or some people saw omens, like a ghostly clue into your future husband. This tradition is another eerie one. Victorians were obsessed with death, probably because they had so much death involving things like illnesses, plagues and poor living conditions. To think that they even relied on the dead to predict their romances is so macabre. Bit different to looking for your future partner in a bar or on a dating app in the 21st century, isn't it?

Lupercalia (13th-15th February)

For this festival, we are going all the way back to the Roman times. Lupercalia was held on the 15th February, it is an ancient

Roman festival celebrating fertility and purification. The mythical founders of this festival were two brothers named Romulus and Remus, who were raised by a she-wolf after they were abandoned by their parents. It sounds incredibly romantic but it's in fact incredibly bloody...

Most men in the festival would strip naked and sacrifice either a goat or a dog. These animal sacrifices were placed with groups of Roman priests, who would smear other people's foreheads using the animal blood and washed off with goat's milk. After the sacrifices, the men would run around, whipping any women close enough with "thongs" (freshly cut goat skin) in a "playful" manner. If you were whipped it was a sign of good luck and fertility. Apparently, this is the only time that they would ever sacrifice a dog, as it's used as a symbol of the she-wolf that saved the brothers.

On a slightly lighter note, the men would also choose a random women's name from a jar, which meant that they were coupled with them for the duration of the festival. Often, the couples would stay together until the next festival, many falling in love and getting married. The festival would also include a lot of food and drink. Romans were particularly fond of their red wine! The festival lasted until the 5th century where it was eventually banned because of the nudity and drunkenness.

There are ways to celebrate Lupercalia in today's day and age. Now I'm not saying you should go out and sacrifice a goat or a dog. But here's a few little tips and tricks that you can get into, that are still subtle.

- Wear red to subtly symbolise the animal blood in the festival.
- Drink red wine (remember to drink responsibly!)
- Indulge in your favourite foods (I would have so much pasta and pizza!)
- Go on a romantic date with your significant other.

DIY Valloween hacks:

- Instead of spending £20 or more on a designed cup from Etsy, even though I love supporting small shops sometimes I just can't buy a cup that expensive. So, I decided to make my own! Primark released a collection of pastel-coloured cups with lids, so I bought a pastel pink cup which was under £5. I then went to Etsy and bought a small sheet of Valloween stickers from a small shop called "CreaturesLikeUsArt" which featured heart-eyed pumpkins, ghosts holding hearts, a potion bottle, a coffin and a purple bat. I peeled off and stuck the stickers on the cup and voila! You have your own inexpensive Valloween cup!

- Valloween 2022 I decided to make Valloween cookies! I picked up a packet of Strawberry Cheesecake filled cookies from Asda and some cheap little icing tubes. I chose four different designs, one for each cookie. I went with Ghostface, a heart pumpkin, a pink and red candy corn and Pennywise the clown. Now, I am not an artist. I prefer 2D drawings on paper so decorating cookies was a bit different for me. I really enjoyed doing this! It was a challenge but by the end I was proud of the product. Not to mention that they tasted delicious! You can make your cookies or biscuits from scratch or do it like me and decorate ready-made cookies

Springoween

March to May

Dear Springoween,

Oh, how happy I am to see you! You are everything that I didn't know that I needed. You bring peachy pink sunrises, ghost-white snowdrops blooming out of the ground. I have already seen the fairy circles sprouting, the daffodils peeping. The air is warmer, I don't feel like I need to bring a heavy witch's cloak with me outside anymore. Springoween is arriving.

Again, I've always felt indifferent about Spring. I feel like I need to publicly apologise to Winter and Spring. I'm sorry I doubted your capabilities. I'm sorry I doubted your beautiful qualities. I never used to take any notice of Spring. But now I do. The colours, the lightness, the softness of Springoween is like the smell of peaches in the air, or walking across the grass bare foot, feeling the daisies tickling your feet.

Springoween is just so *soft*. I think it's what I need after the harshness of Winterween. Spending all day everyday indoors because it's too cold outside. Springoween is also the perfect time to have picnics, and I **love** picnics. Sitting in a park (or cemetery!) listening to laughing children, the birds speaking to each other in their own secret language, the trees rustling like they're trying to tell us something. All of it is beautiful.

Spring, the season of new life and rebirth. Typically, at Easter you tend to see a lot of baby lambs, baby chicks, baby rabbits. However, another new life was born into my family in March 2021. My beautiful niece, Órla Mhairi. She is the light of my life. She makes our family so happy every day. As I'm writing this it is coming up to her 2nd birthday and I just think where have these two years gone? As the second spooky auntie in the family, Órla and I have shared many kooky adventures together. We've been pumpkin picking twice, I've read spooky picture books with her, we've had autumnal walks in the woods together... maybe one day she'll read this and say "oh, so that's what Auntie Egg was writing!". How Springoween it is that - she calls me Auntie Egg!

Don't be fooled into thinking that Spring is all sunshine and pretty flowers though. This is where the "ween" of Springoween comes into it. Be careful on Easter morning, you might find a pumpkin egg in your basket, or a two headed rabbit peeking in your window! If you hear a knock at the door, it could very well be an Easter witch (yes, they do exist!) carrying a pastel-coloured skull as a peace offering. If you go on a spring walk in hopes of flower picking, stay well away from the woods.

You might come across a haunted cottage; a ghost standing in the window, hidden behind the lacy curtains. The "drip, drip, drip" noise can be heard, from many April showers that have rained down on the cottage, but no raindrops or puddles can be found. You feel a tickling on your face, no it isn't your own hair, it's a silvery soft cobweb that a spider has weaved, and you have walked straight into it. You hear a tap, tap, tapping at the window. Is it a goblin? A dark and evil fairy luring you to your doom or is it simply a tree branch being puppeted by the wind. You may never know. This is what Springoween has to offer. Watch your step...

Springoween: March

World Book Day (3rd March)

In the UK, World Book Day is a charity run day, encouraging children all over the country to read and raising money for children who don't have the facilities to buy their own books. In schools, children are offered £1 book tokens so they can buy any of the £1 books that are released. Schools also celebrate the bookish day, encouraging children to come into school or nursery dressed as their favourite book character.

As a child, I **adored** World Book Day. I loved collecting the £1 books and dressing up as my favourite characters. One year, I was particularly excited when my favourite book series (The Tiara Club, it doesn't sound very Halloween-y, but one of the books was centred around witches and a witch's broomstick!) released a special £1 book called "Princess Megan and the Magical Tiara". I was ecstatic. This was the ultimate costume! I wore my favourite princess dress and tiara and went into school with the biggest smile on my face. This is where my love of Halloween dress-up and costumes comes from.

As I've mentioned before I work in a nursery. I've worked in childcare for many years now and this also gives me the opportunity to dress up. For the children of course! Spooky children's books are the best kinds of books, in my opinion. For this day I want to recommend some costumes that you or your children can wear that are based on my favourite spooky books throughout the years, leading up to secondary school!

Character Costume Ideas:

(Preschool and Primary school)

- **Meg and Mog.** My namesake book! I was always a bit of a conceited child, I loved anything with my name in it. Meg and Mog were one of the first picture books that I remember reading, although from further research these books were first published in 1972! It had simple illustrations, Meg the Witch resembled a stick person, with a pointed nose. A black triangle dress and a pointed witch's hat. She had two familiars; a striped cat called Mog, and an owl called Owl. I would recommend for this costume to wear a simple black dress (you could go 90s retro and wear a bin bag!), a pointy witch hat, black and white striped tights and black dolly shoes. You could even go further and find a cat and owl toy (or puppets) for your familiars! Like most of the books from my childhood, Meg and Mog was adapted into a cartoon, I watched it religiously! It had a very catchy theme song!

- **Winnie the Witch**. Another witchy book, I know! Winnie was more of a different witch to Meg. She lived in a black house with her black cat, Wilbur. Winnie's style can only be described as **chaotic**. She wore a purple coat, a blue dress, a pointy witch's hat decorated with stars, "mad" stripy tights with black boots, "crazy" hair, a red nose and black lips. You could get seriously creative for this costume a la Art Attack style. Buy a plain witch's hat (or make one out of card) and glue on different coloured stars. Use red blush to give yourself a flushed nose like Winnie. Experiment with black lipstick. Create the outfit anyway you want!

- **Funnybones.** The cartoon theme song for this was the theme song for my entire childhood. At the age of 25 I can still recite the first few lines of the book. *"In the dark, dark, house, down the dark, dark, stairs, in the dark, dark, cellar some skeletons lived...".* Thankfully, at Halloween in my nursery I still get to pull Funnybones out of the storybook box and enchant another generation of children with this ghoulish story. I wore this costume for World Book Day 2022. I already had a pair of loungewear that was a skeleton design. It consisted of a black long-sleeved top and jogging bottoms with a skeleton body on the front and down the legs. I used black eyeliner to draw a skeleton mouth and nose (a black triangle) and wore a skeleton necklace that I already owned and my Funnybones enamel pin (Yes, I still can't believe I own one!). This is more of a simpler costume, but it still has a great effect!

- **Mona the Vampire.** For this it was more of the TV show that I enjoyed watching, the cartoon was actually adapted from a series of books released in the 90s. Another funky theme song - why weren't these tunes on the radio? For Mona's outfit she wore a simple school uniform with a red cardigan, a black bow tie, a purple starry cape, vampire's fangs and her hair in Medusa braids. I always wanted to be Mona when I was a kid. Not only did I love her name, but she and her friends were constantly having run ins with scary monsters and getting up to all sorts of hilarious hijinks.

(Secondary School-Preteen and teen)

- **Scream Street.** I feel like I was the only kid who knew about this book series! When Luke turns into a werewolf for the first time, he and his family are moved into Scream Street, home to a weirdly wonderful community of vampires, werewolves, witches, zombies etc. For this costume I would go very simple, and you can dress up as any Scream Street neighbour e.g. werewolf, zombie, vampire etc. It reminds me a little of the classic Universal Horror characters, you could also bring some of the other monsters into it e.g. The Creature from the Black Lagoon, a Mummy etc. These books ended up getting adapted into a stop-motion animation series for CBBC in 2015. I was unfortunately past my time of watching CBBC, so I never got to experience the show.

- **Diary of a Wimpy Vampire.** This was the greatest blend of *Diary of a Wimpy Kid, Twilight* and *Dork Diaries*. Again, a book I feel like I only knew about. For this I would go with casual clothes like jeans and a t-shirt, with a vampire cloak thrown over the top. For authentic purposes you could traumatise yourself by adding some greasy hair, pasty white skin (white face powder) and draw on teenage acne. I also feel like this book was a bit of a one-hit wonder as I only remember it as a standalone novel. It still made an impact on me though; I wouldn't be mentioning it otherwise!

- **My Sister, the Vampire.** I'm going to admit a bit of an embarrassing secret. Even though I am a spooky lover now, in high school I was a particularly uncool geek (not that there's anything wrong with that!). In secondary school I had a few friends who were part of the "emo and goth" crowd. In my mind, they were the coolest people I knew. They were misunderstood and quirky like I was, except they wore a lot more black than I did. I desperately wanted to be "emo" like them. I even attempted to draw manga illustrations like they did and failed miserably. When I was in the school library one day, I discovered a book called "My Sister, the Vampire". It's about an American cheerleader called Olivia Abbott who transfers to a new school and discovers that not only does she have a long-lost identical twin, but her twin is also a vampire. It's *The Parent Trap* and *Twilight* fan fiction nobody knew they needed! For this I would go with goth clothes, fake vampire fangs and pale skin. Or you could go as the human cheerleader twin, with a subtle vampire puncture on the neck? I'll always remember this book as a reminder of my emo friends. They were the best.

- **The Spiderwick Chronicles**.

International Women's Day (8th March)

Salem is unfortunately not the only place that has suffered from witch trials, but from where I'm from (Newcastle upon Tyne) we also have a horrifying history of our own...

Between the years of 1649 and 1650 in Scotland and Northern England, witch trials made their way across the pond. The death toll was rising due to plague and disease; bodies were piling up and people were terrified. They didn't know what to believe anymore, so what did they do? They decided to blame innocent people and burn them at the stake or hang them. It didn't help that the government were diabolical and capitalised off people's fear. There were approximately 612 accusations across Scotland and Northern England.

Scotland

In 1649, the Scottish Witchcraft act was put into place. It basically instilled the death penalty for accusations of anyone who was thought to be a "witch". It led to almost a century and a half of witch hunts across Scotland. Early witch hunts were sanctioned by James VI of Scotland and later James I of England and Ireland. Those convicted of the crime were usually strangled and then burnt at the stake with nothing left to bury. I have to admit, as I'm writing this the tears are streaming down my face. The world that we live in can be so cruel, but to think that people did this is... disgusting.

One of the methods of distinguishing who was a witch was by using a "Scottish Witch Pricker". These were people employed to strip the accused woman, find their "witch's mark" (they believed that every woman had a witch's mark, in which they wouldn't be able to feel pain when touched) and prick them on the mark to obtain evidence for court. Some women were that abused by these methods, if some of the pricks, ahem, *prickers*, were especially cruel and keep on pricking them, they would sometimes confess to a crime they didn't even commit out of pure pain. My heart hurts so much for all those that had to endure this disgusting act.

Thankfully during my research, I've found that in 2021 a group named "Witches of Scotland", have campaigned for almost 2 years for the accused victim's names to be cleared completely. This bill was supported by Nicola Sturgeon, a member of the Scottish parliament! This is a **huge** step in the right direction. Even if it is late, the fact that this has been recognised as a problem and tried to be resolved is amazing. I can only hope that Newcastle follows the path, as they still have a lot to answer for...

Claire Mitchell QC, leader of the Witches of Scotland campaign.

"Per capita, during the period between the 16th and 18th century, we [Scotland] executed five times as many people as elsewhere in Europe, the vast majority of them women. To put that into perspective, in Salem 300 people were accused and 19 people were executed. We absolutely excelled at finding women to burn in Scotland. Those executed weren't guilty, so they should be acquitted."

Northern England

Now unfortunately, these witch trials hit very close to home, *literally*. The Newcastle Witch trials took place between 1649 and 1650. The intense witch trials that were happening in Scotland spilled into England, which brought those evil Scottish witch prickers with them. God, I hate them! The puritan minister in Newcastle, Walter Bruce, shared an interest in witch-hunting. He believed that witches "cursed and killed cattle, fed infant babies to the Devil, and ate the flesh of dead children. Honestly, the nerve! After two women were executed for "being witches" in March 1649, news and stories of "witches" spread far and wide, like a dirty rumour spreading like wildfire across a school. The interest infiltrated parishes from Berwick upon Tweed, Holy Island, Newcastle, and Gateshead. Accusations were thrown about at anyone. A witchfinder was even summoned from Scotland (who was later discovered to be a complete fraud!). More than 300 people were executed in the actual witch trials across Scotland and England. 30 women were accused and arrested in Newcastle, after the town crier was sent into a town by the council, asked for anyone with an allegation to step forward. In court there was "confessions" of demonic pacts with the Devil, as a result of this, 5 women were quickly executed in 1649. Overall, 30 people were accused, 28 tragically died from starvation, suicide, or torture. 17 witches were hanged at Gallowgate, 11 died in prison and 2 were freed. 14 women and 1 man were hanged on Newcastle's Town Moor. This specific group were buried in unnamed graves at St Andrew's Church on Newgate Street. Hauntingly, in 2008, there was a period of heavy rain, and the bones of the witches actually resurfaced.

The last two details will haunt me forever. I obviously live in Newcastle. I have walked down Newgate Street so many times in my life. I frequent The Gate cinema and have done since childhood. When I was a child, I never knew that The Gate cinema used to be Newgate Prison. I never knew that "witches" were buried in the churchyard that had pretty flowers growing in Spring. I also have walked across the huge stretch of land that is the Town Moor. Most bizarrely, every year in June, a travelling funfair called "The Hoppings" arrives on the Town Moor for a week and a bit. It was always a childhood tradition to visit the fair; go on the rides (the Magic Mouse was always a favourite of mine), buy a sugar dummy, hot dog, stick of candyfloss etc, and enjoy walking around in the sunshine (when it wasn't raining! Ah yes, the Hoppings is also cursed with rain every year, literally). But now that I know this history, it doesn't necessarily put me off going, but it definitely puts things into perspective.

The Present

Now, you're probably wondering why I'm mentioning this on International Women's Day. I just wanted to say I am not discounting the deaths and torture of the men that were murdered in these trials. They are victims in this just like everyone else. Unfortunately, approximately 84% of the accused witches were women. This is why we need to remember. Remember these poor souls who were tortured and burnt and pricked. Who were dumped and forgotten in unmarked graves, with no memorial. No apologies or pardons (apart from the witches in Scotland now thankfully). Ripped away from their families and loved ones forever.

For me, I want to spread this story **far and wide**. Just like the stories of accusing witchcraft, I want to spread the story of these people all over. They deserve better! They deserve apologies and a proper memorial. Their families and their descendants also deserve apologies. I would be beside myself if I discovered that a great relative of mine was accused of being a witch. It isn't fair to anyone. I know I've tried to keep this book light-hearted and fun, but it's so important to raise awareness of issues like this. We need to remember them.

Newcastle Witch Trials

So, let's review: **Newcastle Witch Trials, many executed, hanged, and buried in unmarked graves. The following executions took place in 1649 on the Newcastle Town Moor, which gives Gallowgate in Newcastle its name. Remember them!**

1. Mathew Bulmer; hanged and burnt for witchcraft.

2. Isab' Brown; hanged for witchcraft.

3. Margret Maddison; hanged for witchcraft.

4. Ann Watson; hanged for witchcraft and using magic to have her 'wicked way' with a Lord.

5. Elleanor Henderson; hanged for witchcraft.

6. Elleanor Rogers; hanged for witchcraft.

7. Elisabeth Dobson; hanged for witchcraft.

8. Mathew Bonner; executed for wizardry and shape shifting.

9. Mrs Elisabeth Anderson; hanged for witchcraft.

10. Jane Hunter; hanged for witchcraft.

11. Jane Koupling; hanged for witchcraft.

12. Margret Brown; hanged for witchcraft.

13. Margret Moffit; hanged for witchcraft.

14. Eleanor Robson; hanged for witchcraft & bloodletting.

Release of Scream 6 (10th March)

"Still alive, I don't wanna just survive. Give me something to sink all my teeth in. Eat the devil and spit out my demons. Still alive, already died a thousand times... Chasing the ghosts that would haunt me at night, facing my past cause I'm up for the fight."

Demi Lovato - Still Alive.

Scream 6 was released on this date in March 2023, I didn't get to watch it until the Easter Holidays though. I had been ill during the holidays, but once I got better, I decided to take myself on a "solo cinema date" to go and see the film. Personally, this was a big deal for me. I enjoy spending time by myself, but activities such as eating out or seeing a film in the cinema was something I avoided. I decided to take a leap and go to the cinema alone, which was actually such as boost in my confidence!

I was nervous at first, especially when I was asking for the ticket I stumbled over my words slightly, but once I was in the screen and found my seat, I felt so much better! I had bought and snuck in a McDonalds (very sneaky!) and enjoyed that as I watched the trailers before the film. When it started, I was completely sucked into the film.

Overall, I really enjoyed Scream 6. It was a great follow up to Scream 5. I can see this new legacy of Scream being a trilogy within the franchise, as the first 3 films were. Scream 5 and 6 combines being for a new generation and still showing appreciation for the "OG" fans. This film specifically felt like the style of Scream 2, when they were in college and Ghostface once again makes an ugly appearance.

The film felt elevated and more stylised, but not in a pretentious way. We still had our "core four" with a few new additions to the cast. We had our red herrings and suspicious characters, with Gale Weathers still holding her legacy title, although she was holding on a by a thread for some of it! I personally love Tara, Sam, Chad and Mindy. They're the perfect continuations of past legacy characters (relative(s) of the first Ghostface, Billy and niece and nephew of our resident horror expert, Randy). They hold their own in the film and are actually very likeable and well-rounded!

The suspense in this film was incredibly intense and the chase scenes were also even better than the first film. I literally could not breathe during the ladder scene. The ending to that was so tragic! The setting was also fantastic. I loved the wider space of running around New York, and also the "showdown" setting of the abandoned movie theatre was so perfect for all of the many film references within the franchise.

The film did a great job at throwing you off who Ghostface actually was. I suspected some but not all of them... I also really enjoyed the return of Kirby and her arc within the film. Again, she's a character from my least favourite Scream film, but it was nice seeing her being reintroduced to the franchise and I hope to see her again in future Scream films!

Sam and Tara (alongside Sidney and Gale of course, and if Tatum had made it to the end of Scream 1!) are my favourite Scream and horror final girls! They're perfect for the new generation that are watching. They're bad-ass sisters who have been through so much together. I love the way they protect each other but also argue just like real sisters do. I want to be a Carpenter sister! Minus the serial killer Dad of course!

We Scream for Ice-Cream

A dessert café in town, that I have visited before, actually released a special Scream-themed ice-cream sundae for the film's release. I was so excited! In the UK, we don't normally get any special merch or release events for anything horror or Halloween-related (some have begun happening in recent years) so this was a big deal!

The day before Mother's Day I took my Mam down for a meal in Wetherspoons and then to go and try the ice-cream afterwards. My Mam loves ice-cream just as much as me so we both thoroughly enjoyed it! The sundae itself consisted of 2 scoops of coconut gelato, vanilla soft serve and lots of strawberry sauce. It also came with the Creams wafer and a little Scream 6 flag stuck in the ice-cream!

I'm a bit of a foodie, so reviewing this was super sweet! It was a **bloody** good ice-cream (get it?) and I can't believe that I actually finished the whole thing! The glass dish seemed endless and kept going! My Mam also enjoyed it as well, she even said it was as good as a McFlurry, which is a big compliment!

Scream Gift Guide

For the release of Scream 6 I decided to head onto Etsy once again to buy myself some Scream merch from the films. Here are those items!

- Ghostface necklace and pin (from *SalemSisters*). I realised that I don't actually have any pieces of Ghostface jewellery! I bought this adorable mini Ghostface necklace to wear to see the film, as well as this "scary movie" pin in the shape of a popcorn bucket.
- Stab VHS tape (from *Classicmoviesstudio*) Stab is a unique and ironic part of Scream that I personally love. I mean, it's a horror franchise within a horror franchise! I feel like it doesn't get the appreciation that it does. A VHS tape is a unique ornament to display in your house, I loved the way this was designed, with authentic blood splatter!
- Bookmarks (from *A Bookish Boutiques* and *KBV Designs*). You know by now that I love a good bookmark! I bought these two, one with Randy's rules on and the other in the shape of a knife with Ghostface within it. The knife bookmark will look particularly cool sticking out of a book!
- Stab keyring (from *Sinister Gifts*) Another tribute to Stab, a keyring! Perfect spooky addition to your car keys, lanyard etc.
- Tote bag and t-shirt (from *Dead Sketch*) I actually met the lovely artist Dead Sketch, twice at two different markets! Her artwork is amazing; her spooky designs obviously

captured my attention! Again, I realised I didn't have a Ghostface t-shirt, and Dead Sketch did a tote bag and t-shirt deal!

- Ghostface print (from *Boo Fang Designs*) I already have a pink Eddie Munson print from this shop, so I couldn't resist when I saw a pink Ghostface print, horror girlies love pink too!

My ranking of the Scream franchise

I recently binged the Scream franchise so that I could get up to date in preparation for the sixth film. It was the first horror movie franchise that I've genuinely really enjoyed and became invested in. I thought I would rank where I personally think each film is placed in order from best to worst.

1. Scream. Obviously, I had to place the first film in first place. It paves the way for the rest of the series! It's our first introduction to the characters, and our first introduction to the core three (Sidney, Gale and Dewey) who are the heart of this franchise. I also really have a soft spot for Randy and Tatum. If Randy hadn't of told them all the "Horror Movie Rules" they would definitely have struggled, they did anyway but they would have struggled even more. Tatum was the perfect side character, but when you notice how much of a good friend she was to Sidney, her tragic demise makes it even more heart-breaking. She definitely deserved to be the final girl with Sidney. Also controversial, but I am obsessed with Billy and Stu. Here is where I confess that I have a **huge** celebrity crush on Matthew Lillard (Stu Macher) which stems from watching the live action Scooby Doo as a child religiously! Matthew's portrayal of Stu is so erratic compared to Billy's silent, scary demeanour. The killer reveal is also **excellent**. It seems so obvious from the beginning, but even so it's still a jaw drop moment. The first Scream really has it all. Comedic lines, suspense, romance, gory kills, and the 90s nostalgia!

2. Scream 5 (2022). Yes, I am putting the second most recent film in second place. It's also a recent watch for me. It was the last film I watched before watching the sixth film, but I honestly enjoyed it the most. In my opinion it is the perfect homage to the franchise. It discusses the new concept of "requels" (films that come out years after the originals but include legacy characters and rebooting the storyline with new characters) and has some seriously gory kills. I really enjoyed the new cast of characters. Most of the new characters were relatives of legacy characters e.g. niece and nephew of Randy, daughter of Billy Loomis, son of Deputy Judy Hicks (Scream 4) and even a side character randomly relating to Stu Macher. They even bring back the actual legacy characters e.g. Sidney, Dewey and Gale and I loved seeing them interact with each other once again. I also loved the mentions of the "Stab" franchise, which is the fictional horror franchise within the Scream franchise, based on the killing spree that happened in the first film. It makes the film even more nostalgic. I also love the dedications to Wes Craven, who directed the first four films. They named one of the new characters after him, even when they have a party to commemorate the murder of the character Wes, they raise a glass to him and touchingly, according to Dead Meat, the audio is actually vocal cameos of various Scream actors from the series including Matthew Lillard, Jamie Kennedy, Hayden Panettiere (Scream 4), Henry Winkler, Adam Brody and Drew Barrymore. And yes, it made me ugly cry. Now the actual reveal of this film's Ghostface isn't my favourite, but I did enjoy their own "Billy and Stu" scene, they played them very well.

3. Scream 2. I have to say, I did enjoy this instalment, but again, it isn't extremely memorable. It felt a bit like Scream: College Edition. Sidney Prescott is now in college (America's version of university) and has a familiar friendship circle. Her boyfriend, sassy best friend, goofy

side friend, Randy back as the film-obsessed goofball etc. She's just trying to survive, still scarred from the events of the first film when Ghostface starts targeting her again. The film brought back also Cotton, who was the man wrongly accused of killing Sidney's mother in the first film. I quite liked his involvement in the film towards the end.

4. Scream 3. This film was definitely different from the first two. The characters were getting older and heading in different directions. The journey that we had been on so far was tumultuous to say the least. I like how this brought in more of the arc of the Stab films. This film focused on the fictional filming of one of the Stab films, and the real life Ghostface decides to attack the actors that are working on that film. The film felt quite "meta" with actors within the film playing characters in the film based on the story within the film… a bit confusing but you get used to it! Now the Ghostface reveal in this film was my least favourite. I liked the idea of it, but it would have helped if Sidney actually knew who they were. The whole point of these Ghostface reveals is that it's a total "Scooby Doo", person behind the mask style reveal ("Not Old Man Winkle, the sweet gardener next door!"). They're always someone that Sidney knows or is associated with. And although Ghostface was *related* to Sidney, she has no idea who he was! It just could have been done better.

5. Scream 4. This film gets a lot of love from the fans, I'm sorry to disappoint, but I do not like this instalment. I just felt like it was trying to be the first film again. Obviously, it was going in the direction of Scream 5, with a new cast of younger characters as the main roles with legacy characters in the background. It could have been great, but it was not. There was just something about it that did not stick with me. It might have been the characters, none of them (apart from Kirby) were particularly likeable or had a well-rounded character. I think the Ghostface reveal was a second first for the franchise (not the first female) but

again, it felt like Scream 3 with another relation of Sidney's. At least this time around we definitely weren't expecting it. Although, Scream 4 definitely influenced Scream 5's Ghostface duo as they felt very similar to each other. Overall, I didn't like this film, but it's nice that it's there and paved the way for the new instalments. It was also sadly, the last film that Wes Craven ever directed in the franchise before he passed away. RIP Mr Craven.

Horror story: Cabin Fever

No, I'm not talking about the film, unfortunately. This is a real-life tale that happened in 2022, when I really experienced cabin fever (just without any drastic measures). It was like reality was mirroring fiction, in a scary way. Although now, it isn't too bad.

For the second time I caught Covid. Yes, second time. The first time I had it was in the dark year of 2020, and I managed to avoid it for months until I caught it again in 2022. I thankfully didn't experience bad symptoms, only cold and flu symptoms but I lost my taste and smell once again. For someone who loves food, losing their taste and smell is torture!

I was experiencing a typical day in isolation. I was lounging around in comfy clothes, not being able to breath out of my nose. I was most likely watching television and scrolling on my phone like the typical millennial that I am. When all of a sudden, we heard a click in the house, a loud click. My television switched itself off, I heard my dad say that his computer had turned off. My family was collectively confused. If it was a power cut, then surely the rest of the street were affected? My mam went to check on our neighbours to see if they were experiencing the same thing as us. Oddly enough, all of their electronics were working fine. It was only our house that was affected. We panicked. My phone was slowly dying on me, the heating vanished, we couldn't cook hot food or even have a cup of tea!

Being the sensible person that my mam is, she immediately tried to ring an electrician, British Gas, anyone that could save us. Nothing was available. It was like being in the Stanley Hotel from *The Shining*. We were isolated. I was **literally** in Covid isolation so I couldn't even leave the house. Thankfully, our neighbours are absolute angels. Our lovely neighbour Margaret offered to charge our electronics in her house e.g., our phones and then pass them back to us. My sister came and visited later (I obviously kept a sensible distance from her) and tried to help as much as she could.

It didn't feel like a bad situation at first. Of course, people have it so much worse than we do. It started to feel bad as the sun went down. It was still early Spring so it wasn't warm just yet. We had no heating, so things got frosty very quick. We had no lights, so as soon as sun set our house switched itself off. The house was cold and dark. I had a very uncomfortable sleep that night, remember, I still had Covid during all of this!

28 hours later, PowerGrid came out to our house to try and sort the situation. It seemed that it was a problem **underneath** our porch, which was strange. We had no idea how it happened and were just as confused as the technicians. Along with PowerGrid, they brought a generator with them. I had never seen a power generator before. It genuinely looked like an army tank. They "plugged" it into our house to give us electricity while they were figuring out how to fix the current problem. We finally had heating, lights, even WIFI! It was heavenly. The only thing I was upset about with having no electricity was realising they were taking "Shaun of the Dead" off Netflix (remember, I watched it every day in January!) and I was able to watch it one last time, thanks to our new housemate!

To distract myself during the day before PowerGrid came and saved us, I decided to read some spooky books. As I mentioned it was still cold outside, it also started snowing. It really did feel like "The Shining". I sometimes enjoy feeling like this. I like to pair whatever I'm reading with how I'm feeling, what the weather is like, what time of year it is (hence my themed reads for each month!). Since it was cold and dull, I thought I'd read some spooky books to liven the day up. I read two books that I had ordered and received recently. They were "The Halloween Moon" and "Shadow Glass". The first book was a middle-grade Halloween hijinks style adventure, that reminded me of stop-motion animation films such as *ParaNorman* and *Coraline*. The second book was a love letter to 80s puppet fantasy films. Very different in terms of genre, but I ended up reading both of them in a day!

57 days we lived with a generator on our driveway. Along with the generator it came with a "sound barrier" because when it was plugged in it made a lovely constant humming sound, a bit like a car engine, **24 hours a day**. I had broken sleep for nearly two months. We also had a **security guard** who came and watched the generator for a few hours a day and even overnight, because apparently, they are worth a lot of money and people will try to steal it! It was like living in alternate universe. I would go to work, come home and it would be sitting there. I was thankful for it being there, I was just wished it was a little quieter! Weirdly enough, when it was eventually gone, I actually missed the noise that it made!

Spring Faeryween...

Dear Faeryween,

When I was a child, faeries followed me everywhere I went. Not in the literal sense of course. In my imagination, they fluttered all around me. They followed me to school, they perched on my shoulder during lessons, they poured out of the pages of the books that I read. To be fair, all I read until the age of 9 was faery books, so it was of course obvious that the faeries lived in every book I read. Folded between the pages, their little wings poking out, ready for me to open them and to be let out into the world.

It was ironic, when I eventually switched to more "grown up" books, I began reading Jacqueline Wilson and the first book I read of hers was a book about a girl called Violet, who was fascinated by faeries. It was called "Midnight" and it was lent to me by my best friend, Bethanie. I could write pages and pages about the books I loved in my childhood, but I think that's a story to save for another book...

You're probably thinking, this is meant to be a Halloween guide, not a faery guide! First of all, I don't exclude. Faeries fit right into the spooky, supernatural world that I love so much. They flitter among the mushrooms and the toads; they spread their magic across the gloom and bring light to dark corners of the world. Nowadays, a love of faeries is known as "fairy core" and fits into the witchy, cottagecore aesthetic that has become so popular on social media.

So, what do faeries and witches have in common? I'm glad you asked! Through research I've found the most plausible reason is their love of nature. Plants, flowers, herbs, mushrooms, the moon, all these elements' links witches and faeries together. And of course, they were both magical beings in their own rights. Who knows, maybe witches consulted faeries during their magical practices? Sending faeries to the farthest corners of the forest to collect their herbs and bring them back, fluttering through the open window of their cottage, dropping the herbs into the bubbling cauldrons for their witch friends.

That's why I wanted to include faeries in this book. This section is essentially stepping temporarily through a faery door into dreamy, ethereal wonderland. Don't worry, you might still spot a mushroom or a pumpkin in the forest. Even bats and crows frequent this land too! While you're here, I highly recommend dropping by our pond, if you catch them on a good day the toads will happily sing you a song!

This section is for little Megan, who just wanted to live among the faeries and read faery books for the rest of her life. This is for you, kid!

Spring Faery Fun Day (21st March)

I had not heard about this "holiday" before researching! Spring Faery Fun Day is an American holiday, celebrating the lightness of spring and the appearances of mythical fairies. The fairies have awoken from their long, winter slumber. They're stretching their little arms, brushing the frost from their hair, wondering what happened. And then they realise, it's finally Spring! The busiest time for fairies. Spring fairies are the first seasonal fairies to arrive in the forest. It's the perfect time for spells and enchantments, bringing spring flowers to life, painting the sky with blush pinks and sugary sherbet yellows.

Welcoming Spring has actually been a common activity for many years! In some cultures, people would perform rain dances to welcome spring and in Gloucester they would (and still do) roll wheels of cheese down a hill! It's an annual race that first started in 1826, it happens on the Spring Bank Holiday on Cooper's Hill. I know this isn't very fairy-like, but I'm a huge cheese lover, so I had to mention it! Although, I'm sure there are some fairies that make cheese, or look after cows... I'm going off on a cheesy tangent!

The appearance of fairies themselves has been discussed for centuries. The story of the Cottingley Fairies was the first case of "sighted" fairies in history, caught on camera! The series of photographs were captured by two young cousins, Elsie Wright and Frances Griffiths in 1920. The story has been debated for so many years, whether it was actually real or not. To this day, it's unclear as to whether it was true or not. A lot of people say that they were faked photos, drawn and staged by the two girls. But I think that they were 100% real, and people should have believed them!

To really get into the spirit of fairies, here is a list of some fairy activities that you can do, not just on this day, but all year around! The point of the Faeryween section is to work fairy magic into your everyday life. Embrace your fluttery fairy wings and fly high!

- Make fairy bread or fairy cakes. Or, if you aren't much of a baker, you can always just buy these as an afternoon tea snack! Fairy bread is the easiest thing to make, all you need is bread, butter and sprinkles! Always remember to leave some as an offering to your fairy friends!
- Create a plant pot fairy garden. This can also be known as a "fairy altar". Collect natural materials like leaves, stones, tree bark etc. You can make little fairy furniture for your fairies to sit on, anything to make them comfortable! But don't forget to keep it as natural as possible.
- Fairy spell jar. Similar to the fairy altar, natural materials in a jar, with your intended spell of something that you want to manifest. Include a crystal that also brings your intentions and wishes. You could also downsize this and make it portable but putting it in a little organza bag that you can take with you!
- Fairy garden tea party. Ah yes, another tea party! A classic in any child's spring day. All you need is a picnic blanket, some cute snacks, add fairy dolls to accompany your tea party. This would be great to do if you have any children!
- Create a fairy journal/diary. This will chronicle any sightings you might see, spells and rituals that you may practise. It gives you a chance to be as creative as possible. You can write about new spring flowers that you've noticed and any other wildlife.
- Go on a fae nature walk. Going on a nature walk can do wonders for your state of mind. Whenever I need to 'clear my head', or just need some 'space', I love going for a walk, either in my local park or nearby nature reserve. Hearing the birds sing, soft sounds of the breeze in the trees,

heavenly! Also keep an eye out for fairies, and make sure the environment is to their liking - pick up any rubbish!

Melanie Martinez: fae music...

When I was in college, I discovered an artist named Melanie Martinez. She had been on The Voice in America and now was a record-selling artist. Her style of music is so individual! Her songs seemed sugary sweet, but they told dark and twisted stories with real-life messages. She performed as a character called Crybaby who was, you guessed it, she was a cry-baby! Her first album told the story of Crybaby's first years of life as a baby and a toddler in a cruel world. She told off boys who "mansplained" to her in *Alphabet Boy*, got kidnapped and then outsmarted a werewolf in *Milk and Cookies*, enjoyed a creepy carnival ride in *Carousel* (which was featured in the opening credits for American Horror Story: Freak Show!). She lived in a pastel pink world, with scary situations.

Her second album named "K12", which stands for kindergarten through to Grade 12. Crybaby is now starting school, and each song tells the story of what happens to her in that Grade. She deals with bullies on the bus in *Wheels on the Bus*, fake friends at school in *Lunchbox Friends*, body image issues in *Strawberry Shortcake*, getting ill at school in *Nurse's Office*, dealing with creepy teacher-student relationships in *Teacher's Pet*. It chronicles her journey into becoming a teenager and although a lot of the stories are fictional, some of the messages relate to Melanie as a person. Like in *Show and Tell*, some of the lyrics speak out Melanie's life in the public eye and constantly being judged for everything she does. Melanie even made a film on top of this album, an eerie musical where we see the story of K12 unfold. It's free to watch on YouTube, Melanie really is a gem.

At the end of K12, Crybaby left our world as we knew it (I won't spoil how!) and now she is *"back from the dead"* metamorphosed as a quadruple-eyed, pink pixie-like fairy! Her new album "Portals" was released on 31st March, with her first song "Death" having its music video debut on the 24th of March. I really love the direction that Crybaby's journey has gone in! I wasn't expecting it, but it's nice to see how much Melanie has grown as an artist and a storyteller that she can take a risk and go off on a different route. We still have Crybaby, but she is now a spiritual being rather than the mischievous 'toddler' that we once knew. I really love when artists tell stories through their music. Melanie is the definition of that. She's a poet, the creepy world that she has created reminds me of the Tim Burton world, but pinker!

Portals is full of mystical and ethereal songs such as "Moon Cycle", "Nymphology", "Faerie Soiree", "Spider Web", "Milk of the Siren" etc. The new world that she has created is very fairy-core with mushrooms, flowers, bugs, people with soft animal masks etc. If you want to listen to fairy music, I definitely recommend this album! I can't wait to see her creativity develop as we see more music videos for the rest of the album!

The Tale of the Brownie...

There once was a little Brownie. She was helpful, polite and eager to please. She did jobs with her fellow Brownies and was overseen by two friendly Owls that supported and guided the Brownies through their different tasks. This Brownie was me! I joined the Brownies around the age of 8 or 9. The club meetings were held at my local church, just five minutes down the road from me. It was a cosy affair! I remember many a light, spring evening walking home from Brownies with my older sister or my Mam. My cousin also used to go to Brownies for a little while so on some nights she would come back to my house for tea.

I had a sash filled with my patches that I earned, I still have my old Brownies annuals that I collected in the loft, and I even remember inheriting a vintage Brownie handbook from my older sister as she had also done it before me. In America,

Brownies are also known as "Girl Scouts" and they also have "Cubs", "Boy Scouts" etc. The younger version of Brownies was "Rainbows" before you move up to Brownies and then you graduate from Brownies into Girl Guides. My sister was a Brownie and a Girl Guide, but I just did the Brownies. I have very fond memories of being in the Brownies. Cosy, carefree memories of being a child and not having to worry about every little thing. I just had to work towards earning my patches for my sash, which was easy enough! But hold on, I'm getting ahead of myself!

Brownies were originally named "Rosebuds" and were founded in 1914 by Lord Baden-Powell. Girl Guiding was already an existing association, and it gained interest by the younger sisters of Girl Guides and Scouts, who also wanted to join. Therefore the "Rosebuds" were born! They eventually decided that they weren't keen on the name Rosebuds, so the sister of Lord Powell suggested "Brownies" which were "helpful little creatures" in a fairy story that she enjoyed. The name stuck! Around this time, WW1 began, the Brownies made small helpful deeds to contribute to the society during this turbulent time.

The Brownie promises to "always do my best: to do my duty to God and serve my Queen, and to help other people and to keep the Brownie Guide Law.". This is why the name Brownies fits so perfectly. Brownies were known as solitary, home fairies that are a little gnome-like. They did charity work, they helped their community, they were taught lots of practical skills such as cooking, baking, creating things, taught how to be a good citizen etc. Most of all, they were **helpful**! Brownies have changed so much over the years, but the law remains unchanged. Looking back, I'm so glad I joined the Brownies. It taught me how to be a good person!

Not only did we learn practical skills, but we also did a lot of fun and silly activities. I remember doing a "summer musical", like a mini recital where we had to learn songs from the musical *Grease*. Nothing says summer more like belting out *Summer Lovin'* totally out of key! We also went to Jesmond Dene on one occasion, for a ceremony of some sorts. Jesmond Dene is one of my favourite places on this planet. I can't remember what we were there for, but I remember standing in front of the breath-taking waterfall for most of it.

If you're wanting to follow fairies, I recommend joining (if you're the right age, being a Brown or Snowy Owl leader was also something that intrigued me!) or researching about the Brownies. Fairies, mushrooms, owls, nature.... You can't get anymore fairy core than that!

Types of fairies you might meet...

I recently read a book called *"Fairy Magic"* by Aurora Kane. It's a handbook on spells, enchantments, and everything you need to know about fairy lore. There's so much that I didn't know about fairies! This includes types of fairies within every culture. Each culture has their own fae lore with lots of fairy characters. I thought I'd list some here, not everyone of course, there's thousands! These are from many different cultures across the world.

- *Menehune*. This is a Hawaiian dwarf race, known for being mischievous in nature. They are known to inhabit tropical forests.
- *Mazzamurello and Monaciello*. These guys are Italian elves, known as the 'cousins' to our Irish Leprechaun.
- *Will-o-Wisp*. This is an elemental fire fairy, haunts marshy bogs.
- *Melusine* (this happens to be the name of my DnD character!). They're a French sea spirit of a young girl.
- *Trasgu*. This is a Spanish sprite, similar to the Irish Leprechaun. A very loyal household keeper.
- *Peri*. These are Persian trickster fairies. Very cheeky, known for moving and hiding human objects.

- *Chin Chin Kobakama*. This is a Japanese house fairy whose main characteristic is that they love cleanliness.
- *Fairy Godmother*. Popular character in children's fairy tales, granter of wishes and protector from harm.

How to attract/spot a fairy:

- Fairies **love** offerings. They're particularly drawn to ribbon, honey, berries, cream and butter, beer (!), birdseed, fallen leaves, clean water, bread and cake, seeds. If you're creating a ritual, always remember to leave a little something special out for the fairies to show your appreciation of them.
- Fairy portals are recognised as a "fairy ring" which is a circle of mushrooms, or a "fairy door" which can you find at the bottom of a tree. Don't try and block a fairy door or disrupt a fairy ring, you will break the fairy's respect, and they are vengeful!
- They dwell in marshes, forests, gardens, fields, ponds, lakes and rivers. They are the keepers of flowers and know when they have been tampered with.
- Fairies also work by the *Wheel of the Year*, so if you practise fae witchcraft, don't forget to incorporate the fairies into your Sabbat spell work. Midsummer in particular is the most powerful night of the year for them.
- On the off chance that you have an evil fairy on your case, repel it by using iron, rowan trees, herbal remedies, offerings, salt. Do not eat fairy food left by them. They prefer to give, receiving can be risky!

The Faerie Witch Trials

So not only could you be accused of being a witch, but they also did not like if you dabbled with the faerie folk either! A lot of these Faery Witch Trials occurred in Italy, around the time of the 15th century. Faeries and witches have been linked for thousands of years, because of their use of elemental and natural magic.

"The Fisher wife of Palermo" was a well-known fairy trial case back then. The wife of a fisherman was accused of being a witch, and she told them that she had to ability to leave her body and meet with elves whenever she liked. She signed a contract from the King and Queen of Elves, as they promised her many riches. She was actually **released**! They believed that her fairy faith was strong, and that she was not involved with the Devil. This might be seen as a relief for her; however, they passed off her talk of faeries as "dreams".

In Scotland in the sixteenth century there was two other cases of accused witchcraft. A witch accused in Scotland claimed that she had met the Queen of the Faeries. She confessed that the Queen taught her and other witches how to fly on beanstalks! Her confession is actually the most notable case we have from this time period. Her name was Isobel Gowdie. Bessie Dunlop from Lynn said that she had a spirit familiar named Tom Reid, who was the ghost of a soldier. She also confessed to being able to visit the Elf-Land through an ancient cave.

It seemed that people weren't bothered by faeries. They've been a part of folklore for so many centuries, so the Church didn't care. However, as soon as any mention of the Devil was brought up, all hell broke loose, literally! If you were believed to have worked with the Devil or used witchcraft to harm others, you were tortured and executed. If you mentioned that you had been in contact/seen faeries and used spell work with them, the Church passed you off as having a mental illness or having silly dreams. In some cases, if you confessed this while on trial, you could be released but not pardoned. It makes me sad that no matter what those poor women did, they could not prove their own innocence. Nobody believed them! And to just say they had a "mental illness" is so cruel. Just think how many lives could have been saved if they had said that they saw faeries...

I'm so glad that modern Witches/Wiccans are reclaiming their 'witchiness'. They're fighting for all those women who were told they were 'silly' or 'dreamy'. They were nothing more than delusional or manic. You might have heard of the phrase "We are the Granddaughters of the witches you couldn't burn". I see it used a lot on witchy t-shirts or stickers. A lot of people have said that it's "cringe", but I like it! The "granddaughters" have reclaimed that power that their grandmas lost during the witch trials. Wear your faery wings and your witchcraft with pride!

Reading with faeries...

As I said earlier, I spent my childhood reading fairy books! I read every single book in the *Rainbow Magic* series. I also loved *Felicity Wishes*, *Naughty Fairies* and the *Disney's Pixie Hollow* series. If it featured sparkly fairy wings, I was all about it! I was very into the sparkly dresses, fluttery wings kind of fairies, that when I discovered books about **faeries**, it was a whole other story! Here's some books that I recommend if you are older but still want to read about faeries!

- *Fairy Magic*. This is a handbook that explains different spells, enchantments, types of faeries, fairy history etc. I found the book to be very informative and told in an easy and poetic way. The book itself is also beautiful, a little pastel purple hardcover that I popped my purple amethyst crystal bookmark in!
- *Fairy Spells*. Another fairy non-fiction, tiny little book with information and history of fairies. There was a lot of information in this book, but it really was eye-opening!
- *Emily Wilde's Encyclopaedia of Faeries*. This is a newly published adult book with plenty of fairy core vibes, romance and magic. It's been a very popular book on social media, I heard so much about it I knew that I had to try it!
- *Wings*. This is a YA novel, not in the adult age range like I've mentioned but I still wanted to mention it because I do

love YA books. In the valley of Netflix's *Winx Club* adaptation.

- *A Midsummer's Night Dream*. Everyone knows Shakespeare, has read Shakespeare at some point in their life. This is one of the oldest stories of faeries that I know, in the form of a play.
- *The Fairy Garden*. Not for older readers, but I had to mention this picture book for the stunning illustrations. Reminded me of the books I read as a child, with factual fairy information mixed in to educate young faery witches.

Springoween: April

National Tea Day (21st April)

If you are a British person, there is a very strong chance that you enjoy drinking tea. You might be one of the few that prefer coffee (what are you doing with your life?!) but myself personally, I prefer tea. I like my tea the way the builders have it; milk and two sugars. I've tried to venture into different flavoured teas. I don't think I'm quite as cultured yet.

There are, magically, autumnal flavours of tea that are perfect to drink if you are a lover of Halloween and autumn:

- Pumpkin tea
- Apple tea
- Cinnamon tea
- Ginger tea
- Chai tea

I have yet to dive into these flavours. I'm so used to my milky tea that anything else is entirely foreign to me! If you are a tea connoisseur, you might be very familiar with these flavours, I definitely will try them before I publish this book!

Tea parties/Afternoon tea.

The afternoon tea was apparently established by Anne, the Duchess of Bedford (a close friend of Queen Victoria). She asked for light sandwiches to be brought to her during the afternoon, because she had a "sinking feeling" waiting in between the long gaps between meals. I don't think I've ever identified with anyone more! It was introduced into high London society and became very popular among the posh.

We also know that the "Boston Tea Party" was an American protest happening on 17th December 1773, whether it was a literal tea party or not I still think it's worth mentioning. Adding milk to tea also apparently originates from France, with a Madame de la Sabliere serving it in her famous Paris salon. Milk could be added to poor quality tea to make it taste nicer. It's also said that sandwiches, which Anne wanted brought to her in the afternoons was created by Earl Sandwich (yes, that is his real name!). He was playing cards and didn't want to leave the table to eat. He asked for a serving of roast beef to be placed between two slices of bread, so he could still play cards. Voila, the sandwich!

In modern day, afternoon tea and tea parties are still a classic British custom. It's more accessible and not just for posh folk, but available in many a British café. We've also expanded into more **boozy** themes, with "bottomless brunch", "Drag brunch" and many a themed afternoon tea.

I always feel very civilised when I go to an afternoon tea. When my Mam retired from work, her friends bought her a voucher for an afternoon tea at Jesmond Dene House. It was truly extraordinary! The glossy views of Jesmond Dene outside the windows, the calm and quietness of indoors, nothing loud, just relaxing soft music in the background. We had lovely sausage rolls and little sandwiches (salmon and cream cheese is always my favourite) and the most artisan cakes and eclairs and scones.

Back in 2020, when the government forced us indoors (an absolute dream for introverts!) I held a tea party/afternoon tea in the garden for myself and my Mam. It was around the time of VE Day, so it was 40s/50s themed with a touch of Alice in Wonderland whimsy! I wore a patterned tea dress and an Alice band in my hair, we ate scones, strawberries, mini cupcakes and slices of Battenburg cake. I played a "All Out 50s" playlist on my Spotify, and we felt whisked away back to 1950! The vibes were immaculate.

Whenever I think of a tea party, I always think of the Mad Hatter's Tea Party in Alice in Wonderland. The whimsy, the bizarreness and the actual amount of tea is perfect. Here is an idea for an Alice in Wonderland afternoon tea/tea party, with a horror twist...

Merry Unmurdered Day...

For this tea party you can hold for yourself, family, friends, whoever you like! For the décor of the party, I would stick with classic Wonderland whimsy. Incorporate playing cards, clocks, hearts, diamonds, rabbits, mushrooms and flowers. Whether that's having heart shaped napkins, a little clock on the table or even a mushroom ornament! I would also focus on the colours black, red and white to keep the spirit of the Red Queen alive.

For your menu, present on vintage china (or something similar, search charity shops!) and paper doilies for decoration. An Afternoon tea menu can include sausage rolls, sandwiches, scones, cakes like we've mentioned but keep everything small and light. Keep the cups of tea rolling and if you happen to have a big tea pot, that's even better!

Now this is where things get twisted... If you want to make your party stand out, I will include a "murder mystery" element. Ask each guest to come dressed as a Wonderland character e.g., Mad Hatter, White Rabbit, March Hare etc. Make sure they are also acting in character! Prepare a storyline beforehand so that you (the Game Master) know where the party is heading. As you start the party, one of the characters is suddenly poisoned! Probably from off milk in their tea... The remaining characters have to solve the mystery of how they died and catch the killer before they poison someone else! It's essentially an interactive game of Wink Murder with lots of fun elements!

This kind of tea party gives you freedom to go **wild!** Spill blood if you have to! (I don't condone spilling actual blood though). It reminds me of a real-life game of DnD. Once everyone is sucked into the story and deep into their characters, you can be as creative as you like, and your guests will hopefully have just as much fun as you are! Merry Unmurdered Day everyone...

National Picnic Day (23rd April)

I have always been a huge fan of picnics. It was a classic childhood tradition than ran through my childhood. Even when I was a teenager, me and my cousin had our own picnic tradition. We would go swimming at our local swimming baths, come out and head to the high street. We would go to Sainsbury's and buy a meal deal each, plus a few snacks. We would then go to our local park (which was just outside of the high street) and enjoy the lovely weather while we had our 'picnic'. So, we may not have had the traditional red-and-white checked blanket or the wicker basket, but our picnics were perfect as they were.

Now that I think of myself as practicing in the "pumpkin arts" (living a Halloween lifestyle) I thought it was only appropriate to give you some ideas for ghastly picnics. Before we do that though, I have to share some fun facts about the history and origins of picnics because what is life without fun facts!

- The practice of picnics has French origins, and the actual word may have French roots! The verb "piquer" means "to peck or to pick" and the noun "nique" which means "a small amount or nothing whatsoever". This is speculation of course, but I feel like it's as good an answer as anything!
- The actual creation of the picnic is a bit of a mystery. It seems to have possibly had origins dating back to the French Revolution. However, they started to become their

own thing in the 18th century. It became a pastime of rich aristocracy, usually held indoors in hired rooms. It was certainly more professional than more casual picnics of nowadays! Some picnics could even be compared to a "dinner and dance" with music and entertainment.

- The French Revolution changed everything for these aristocratic picknickers, forcing them to flee to different countries, a lot of them ending up in middle class England. They technically introduced England to picnics! In late 1801, "The Pic Nic Society" was founded. These events were filled with music, dancing, food, and even a play. Each guest was required to bring a dish and six bottles of wine to cover the costs.
- Outdoor picnics were eventually introduced in the United States. American picnics conjure up images of the nuclear family with their wicker basket and checked blanket, skipping to a sunny park and settling on the grass for a hearty picnic.
- In the early 20th century, picnic baskets were introduced. You could hear picnics being talked about in works of fiction such as "The Wind and the Willows" and the "Famous Five" series where food items such as cold chicken and ginger beer were most likely to be found in the simple wicker basket. Picnics have evolved so much over the years; they will continue to change. If you've been looking for a Halloween picnic idea, however, look no further!

How to create your petrifying picnic!

1. Choose your theme. Before you even begin to pick your menu you need to decide what your theme is going to be. Are you going classic Halloween, all pumpkins and bats, or will you go with a specific film? E.g., Hocus Pocus, Casper, Friday the 13th? This can help you decide what kind of food to go with, themed foods are the way to go for sure!

2. Crack the crockery. Now that you have a theme that you are happy with you can start to select some pieces of crockery and a basket or bag to transport your picnic in. If you have any pieces that you already own that you can use I highly recommend using them! Choose a basket or a bag that isn't too heavy to transport your items in and is easy to hold.

3. Create your food menu. This is the most exciting part! Now that you have the theme and your crockery, you can start choosing your food. If you're going for a colour scheme you could go for orange food (pumpkin orange). Or go for Halloween shaped things e.g., pumpkin shaped sandwiches etc. This is definitely not a creepy cookbook so I can't recommend specific recipes, but this gives you the opportunity to be as creative as you like!

4. Your picnic outfit. Of course, you must dress to impress! I love trying different Halloween themed outfits, even on a picnic! Dress to make yourself feel comfortable of course, try and go with the theme as well.

5. Choose your location. Where are you planning on having this picnic? You could have it in the park, in a cemetery (always be respectful of your surroundings), in some pretty woods etc. I would also advise checking the weather as well in case you need any waterproofs. You don't want to end up having a soggy picnic!

6. Light entertainment. Whether or not you're doing this picnic alone or with friends, you can also bring along some entertainment. Make a playlist that you can listen to stick with your theme. If you're alone, you could bring a book with you to read. Reading outdoors is always an atmospheric experience. Just you, the words in the book and the wind whistling through the trees!

My petrifying picnics!

Blood and Honey picnic...

This picnic theme is inspired by the 2023 horror film reimagining of "Winnie the Pooh". Yes, that is a thing that exists! Winnie the Pooh always reminds me of Springtime. A funny little yellow bear running through the woods with his animal friends, chasing butterflies and eating honey... Let's splash blood on it!

To serve your picnic I would go with Winnie the Pooh plates and cups. Places like Asda and Tesco sometimes do ranges where they sell Disney crockery (Asda actually do have a range of Winnie the Pooh picnic items at the moment!). If you could find a Winnie the Pooh blanket to sit on that would also work well.

For food I am focusing on "blood and honey" (don't worry, not actual blood!). For the "blood" I would focus on red food e.g., jam sponge cakes and scones, red apples, berries etc. For the honey I saw people eating honey and cheese crackers (strange combination) but you could give it a try! I do love cheese. For extra red and yellow colours, I'd add other food such as yellow plums, teddy face crisps (for the bear!) and not necessarily red and yellow, but ham and olives are great charcuterie snacks! Lemonade and berry juice are refreshing beverages to go with the theme!

If you want to further the teddy bear's picnic theme you could even bring a Pooh or Piglet plush toy (this would be great if you had young children/nieces or nephews/grandchildren!) and add some spooky accessories to them like a black ribbon around the neck or black sunglasses. Really lean into the macabre! The spookier the better!

Hocus Pocus picnic!

I've named this the Hocus Pocus picnic, but it has a general witchy theme that you can adapt in any way you like! I was inspired by some videos I saw on TikTok to create this picnic idea. A specific TikTok account (@the_huntysaurus) had the most bewitching charcuterie spell books (a charcuterie board in a box that looks like a spell book!) I couldn't resist mentioning!

For the rest of your menu, I would include food such as orange pumpkins (draw a little pumpkin face on the skin of the orange or satsuma!), coffin shaped or witch hat sandwiches (using Halloween cutters, can find them online or during the Halloween season), black pasta, and any other of your favourite spooky snacks that you can make or find. You could even make some witchy cocktails if you're feeling adventurous!

For the décor of your picnic, I'd stick to a black or purple blanket to sit on, add a centrepiece of a cauldron ornament, maybe add some purple flowers for that extra colour and pop some skull heads around and on your blanket because witches love skulls! Crystals can also cast beautiful energies so bring a few crystals for positive energy!

Don't forget to bring your witch hat and broomstick with you! Park your broomstick next to your blanket so you can fly away after you've indulged in your picnic! During the picnic you could also include games and have a witchy playlist playing in the background. This particular picnic is a favourite of mine. Be the witch you were always meant to be!

Easterween (March-April)

Easterween is another "ween" holiday that I am new to. I love that Halloween has managed to bleed into so many other holidays, that people celebrate just as much as they do Halloween. Easterween takes the cute image of bunnies and pastel Easter eggs and completely turns it on its head! It's severed head...

Ghoulish Gift Guide:

Did you think I just had one gift guide to show you? Absolutely not, in this book, gift guides are all year around! I've done extensive research into what to get for Easterween. It was a bit of a tricky holiday, but I think I've *cracked it* (get it?).

- Witch Bunny pin (from *Jennifayire*). There were a few candidates when I was searching for the perfect pin. There was a more folk lore inspired Jackalope inspired pin. I decided to go for this adorable rabbit pin, wearing a witch's hat. I love anything witch-related, so this is perfect to add to my collection.

- Nature Eggs bookmark (from *ButterflynToadstool*). This bookmark isn't necessarily spooky, but I really did enjoy the more natural design. The speckled eggs give me a more "haunted cottage core" vibe that's different to a normal Easter egg.

- Haunted Spring bookmark (from *MaleficaCrafts*) I've bought from this small shop before. Their designs are whimsical and cute, usually featuring ghosts doing different activities. This specific bookmark features two ghosts having a wander down a cherry blossom street. I love the artistry of the flowers featured, one of my favourite parts of spring is all of the flowers blossoming.

- Gothic Fillable Egg (from *Dreamfield Co*) This is a new edition in the gift guide! I normally buy pins, prints, stickers and bookmarks but I saw this and I couldn't resist. If you don't want to buy a regular Easter Egg, I would recommend going for an alternative Easter Egg! You can fill up this egg with your own sweet treats (I'd go for variations of Mini Eggs) so you still have your chocolate intake for the sweet holiday. It also has "Happy Easter" written on in gothic print.

- Spooky Easter stickers (from *The Planner Crypt*) If you have a diary or a planner then these stickers will be perfect to use. It sticks with the colour scheme of blue, purple and black and I love the other sticker sheet of rabid rabbits.

- Bee and Crystal pin (from *FuzziesArtDesigns*) Bees, butterflies, ladybirds are also all part of Springoween. In fact, in May it is World Bee Day! Celebrating bees is very important anyway, they're such a huge part of our ecosystem. This beautiful pin combines witch's crystals and a gorgeous little bee.

Haunting History

It's time to step back into the time machine and travel through history to look at some eerie Easter traditions! Easter is primarily a religious holiday, but it does have spooky origins like a lot of these do. I love that the further I step into history, the more I see the ghost of Halloween leaving its whispery trails throughout time.

Swedish Easter Witches

Yes, you heard that right, **Easter Witches!** This was a particular tradition that I found the most interesting. Obviously, the tradition of trick or treating originated from Irish lore, but it's nice to hear that other countries have their own version.

On Maundy Thursday when Judas betrayed Jesus, it was believed that evil was released into the world, including witches on their broomsticks who supposedly would fly to an island where the devil would welcome them to his court. Since then, children would dress up as "Easter witches" and go door to door wishing people a "Happy Easter" in exchange for sweets and homemade cards.

There are no scary costumes, however. The children wear headscarves and shawls and paint their cheeks rosy-red with freckles. Another part of this tradition is when the children knock on people's door, they recite a rhyme:

"I wave a twig for a fresh and healthy year ahead, a twig for you, a treat for me!" Which has been translated from Swedish. The twigs come from another Swedish Easter activity, when children go out and gather eggs to paint and birch twigs to decorate with feathers. I love hearing that trick or treating is twisted around in different cultures. Trick or treating was always my favourite part of Halloween, it should be encouraged everywhere!

Easter Bonfire

In Germany, they believed that outdoor bonfires would scare off witches. Wow, history really was terrified of witches! They would have these big outdoor fires to try and scare them off, and in Sweden the children would **dress** as them! As Regina George said in *Mean Girls: "why are you so obsessed with me?"*.

The tale of the Jackalope

This isn't necessarily from history, but it is a piece of folk lore. The Jackalope is rumoured to be a species of rabbit, with antlers. It's a cross between a pygmy deer and a killer rabbit. They use their antlers to fight and can be extremely vicious. This is of course a piece of American folklore, particularly "seen" in North America. There are so many stories of American folk stories and their monsters out there. There's the Mothman, Big Foot, The Jersey Devil etc. Another spooky piece of Easterween that keeps the spirit of Easter alive.

The Vampire Rabbit of Newcastle

As I've mentioned before, I was born and bred in Newcastle upon Tyne in the Northeast of England. Although I am proud of where I'm from, I didn't think we had much "spooky" history before I started to research for this book.

Thankfully, during researching I've been exposed to so many spooky pieces of history. I definitely don't need to travel to Salem for some spookiness (it is on the bucket list though!).

Did you know that vampire rabbits lurk in the shadows of Newcastle? If you walk down from Newcastle's Bigg Market towards St Nicholas Cathedral, take a wander around the back of the church, hidden in a little courtyard, you'll find the Vampire Rabbit, a gargoyle perching above the doorway of one of the historic Cathedral Buildings.

Originally the fanged creature was a sandy pink colour, the same as the building, but over the years he has been painted black, with added dribbles of blood for extra effect. Nobody knows quite where the creepy creature came from. Some stories tell of the rabbit being put there to scare off grave robbers as the graveyard was originally situated there. The rabbit has encouraged people to be creative and come up with their own stories of the mysterious bunny.

Once I heard about this phenomenon, I had to go and investigate! I donned my Velma glasses (I already have her haircut!) and took a bus ride into town. Initially I had no idea where it was. Once I did a quick Google Maps search, I wandered around St Nicholas Cathedral. Before I even found the phantom bunny I came across some gravestones that were still standing after all these years. One of the graves even had skull and crossbones illustrated at the top!

When I rounded the corner into the hidden street, I looked up and saw the rabbit I was so excited! There he was, creeping on the doorway. I of course had to take some photos with the rabbit. On the wall next to the doorway was some posters which discussed some historical facts about the area, one of which was the supposed story of the Vampire Rabbit. So, if you live in Newcastle, and don't fancy having the Easter Bunny knocking at your door, visit the Vampire Rabbit instead!

Rabbit Ears OOTD

For a spooky take on a traditional Easter outfit, wear your most gothic outfit with black accessories and add the most pastel pair of rabbit ears you can find! You could also add pastel flowers (whether that's on a necklace or jewellery, on your nails etc). Pastel or pink and purple make-up can also brighten your dark look and pull it in the Easterween direction!

Eat all the eggs!

If you really like eggs, and not just chocolate eggs, these ideas are for you! Decorate hard boiled eggs/craft eggs with spooky designs, horror movie characters, ghosts and pumpkins etc. Depending on how artistic you are there are also stencils and tutorials you can follow online. Cut out holes in soft boiled eggs so that they look like little ghosts (two holes for the eyes and one hole for the mouth). Add black olives to scrambled eggs to look like little spiders! And lastly, have a good old-fashioned egg and spoon race with your creepy eggs or an Easterween egg hunt with terrifying prizes!

Spooky Easter basket

Easter baskets with gifts other than chocolate eggs are a more recent trend I've noticed. I have noticed people creating spooky Easter baskets for friends and family. Use a black basket as your base and add a mixture of spring items, presents picked specifically for your chosen person that they would enjoy. If in doubt, add lots of black and gothic items to keep the creepy theme going!

World Dance Day (29th April)

I am putting it out there right now, I am not a dancer. I never will be a dancer; I have zero rhythm. I like dancing for fun though. It can be a great way to get fit, it boosts serotonin levels and can make you feel happy all around. What's better than dancing to music, than dancing to spooky music? Halloween music is not just reserved for Halloween parties. I have many playlists saved on my phone for different occasions. I listen to them more than I listen to whatever song is playing on the radio!

For World Dance Day you can quite simply listen to your favourite Halloween songs in whatever way you wish. You could put in your earphones and put a playlist on as you're going for a run, or a walk in the park. You could listen to them if you're out shopping or even playing the "main character" and taking yourself out on a solo date. People watching while listening to Thriller can be a fun experience. Or you can have a dance party, with disco lights for added affect.

As well as this activity I thought I'd give you some facts about your favourite Halloween songs, most of them are also my favourites!

- *Monster Mash by Bobby Pickett and the Crypt-Kickers*. This song was released in 1962, surprisingly in August. Originally Bobby (also known as Boris) would sing with a band called The Cordials and on one particular performance he acted out a monologue in the style of horror movie actor, Boris Karloff. They loved the way he performed this monologue, so much so that it led to him composing *Monster Mash*. The dance and song were also inspired by the "Mashed Potato" dance that was sweeping the nation at the time. Originally the BBC banned the song in the UK, claiming that it was "too morbid", but it eventually went to Number 3 in 1973 when it was re-released. The song actually became a bit of a trilogy when he released two other songs, one called "Monsters Holiday" in December 1962, "Monsters Rap" in 1985 and even a whole movie musical was created in 1995. *"He did the mash, he did the monster mash, the monster mash, it was a graveyard mash."*

- *Time Warp dance from Rocky Horror Picture Show*. This dance was part of a scene in the movie musical *Rocky Horror Picture Show* which was released in 1975. According to my Mam, she had a "watch party" of the film with her friends from work, as Channel 4 released it for the first time in the UK. Her friends were apparently shocked; they'd never seen anything like it! I have to admit, when I first saw the film I was very confused by what I was watching! I can now appreciate just how crazy the film is, and the cult following that it has. My older sister is a huge fan of the movie and the musical. The Time Warp is one of my favourite songs in the film, it tells you exactly what the steps are in the song! *"It's just a jump to the left, and then a step to the rii-ight. Put your hands on your hips! You bring your knees in tight, But it's the pelvic thrust, that really drives you insane!"*

- *Everybody (Backstreet's Back) by the Backstreet Boys*. Alongside Thriller, this was another music video that I could not watch as a child, because it scared me! I'm so glad I'm not as much of a wimp nowadays. This song was released in 1997, the year I was born. The concept of the video was created by the Backstreet Boys themselves and was inspired by Michael Jackson's Thriller. The video was set in a haunted house, where their tour bus broke down outside of a haunted house. The boys must spend the night in the house while their bus is getting fixed. They each share a nightmare in which each boyband member portrays a different Universal Monster. These include a Mummy, Dracula, Phantom of the Opera, Dr Jekyll and Mr

Hyde and a Werewolf. I learnt a lot of interesting things while researching. According to sources, Brian's makeup as the Werewolf took 5 and a half hours to do. Nick originally wanted to be the *Creature from the Black Lagoon*. The Special Effects supervisor also worked on familiar horror films e.g., *Candyman* and *Hellraiser III*. The part of this music video that always scared me was the bus driver returning at the end, with a more sinister look.

- *The Wednesday Dance choreographed by Jenna Ortega (Goo Goo Muck by the Cramps).* This is the most recent spooky dance to be released into the world, coming out in 2022. The dance was featured in a scene from the TV show *Wednesday* and happened during the school's ball. Wednesday ends up out of her comfort zone in the school ball, she dances in her own quirky way which ends up impressing her date. One of the most impressive things I found out about this dance was that Jenna Ortega choreographed it herself, using videos of goths dancing in clubs as inspiration. A little Easterween egg that I also love is one of the moves that she does is taken directly from Lisa Loring, who played the original Wednesday Addams in the 60s TV show where little Wednesday teaches Lurch how to dance. I love that she included this move, it is particularly poignant knowing that Lisa unfortunately passed away just a few months after the modern *Wednesday* was released.

- *Thriller by Michael Jackson.* As I mentioned in my Winterween letter, this music video haunted my childhood. The first opening notes would send literal shivers down my spine. The zombies, Michael's wolf face and even the dancing would be enough to make me cry. Vincent Price's chilling voice also spooked the hell out of me. Now that I'm an adult I've gotten over my silly childhood ways and I can appreciate the video for the piece of art that it is. It was released in 1983 and Michael was only 24 years old when he did the song and the video.

It was inspired by the film "An American Werewolf in London" and a remix was used in the trailer for Season 2 of *Stranger Things* (my favourite version of the song!). *"Darkness falls across the land, the midnight hour is close at hand, creatures crawl in search of blood, to terrorise y'all's neighbourhood..."*

What a Wicked Weekend!

Celebrating Halloween all year long is a big passion of mine (hence this book!) but sometimes, you can get very lucky... This weekend in particular (29th-30th April), we have not 1, not 2, not even 3, but **4** spooky events! All four of these events fall onto the same weekend, which means you can have the most spooktacular time celebrating! We have Halfoween, Walpurgisnacht, Beltane (which is technically on the 1st of May, but I still include it as it's the day after, and it happened in 2023 on the Bank Holiday weekend!) and finally we have the Whitby Goth Weekend! Three of these events you can celebrate and modify yourself at home, but the Whitby Goth Weekend is a place to travel to, although I have included some tips to channel the Whitby Goth at home too! It's not often that spooky events happen at the same time so it's great to take full advantage and really lean into the spook!

Halfway to Halloween (30th April)

Not only is 30th April exactly 6 months away from Halloween, but it is also known as "Walpurgisnacht" aka witch's night! These two events also occur the day before Beltane, our 4th seasonal festival of the Wheel of Year, marking the peak of spring and the upcoming summer season! With this trio of events happening so close to each other, it's a Halloween lover's dream!

Halfoween

As I said before, Halfoween is exactly 6 months before Halloween. A lot of people like me choose to celebrate the day in style, choosing to treat it like an early Halloween! The Disney Parks also host a Halfway to Halloween event and a "Mickey's Not-So-Scary Halloween Party" around the time of Halfoween! It is on my bucket list to travel to the Disney Parks and attend these spooktacular events! Until then though here are some simple things you can do at home to celebrate Halfoween!

- Watch your favourite Halloween films. If you're feeling brave, if there's any horror films out currently at the cinema you could also go and watch them!
- Make plans for Halloween. Plan your outfit, any content you want to put out, what you want to read, watch etc. Creates the hype for the best day of the year!
- Have a spooky bubble bath. I always buy the Halloween collection from Lush and end up saving them because they are too pretty to use. Now is the perfect time to use them up in preparation for more spooky bath products!
- Make Halloween snacks. Be creative and cut different shapes out of various foods or if you're like me, I bought 5 bags of Halloween-shaped pasta during October the year before! Have a bowl of comforting Halloween pasta or a hot chocolate in a creepy mug.
- Carve a turnip or go apple-bobbing. You can practise your skills in preparation for Halloween parties!

Walpurgisnacht (30th April-1st May)

Known as the "witch's night" in German and Norse traditions. It is the time when the veil between worlds thins, allowing creatures to pass through and travel to meeting places. The night is apparently named after St Walpurga, who was an English nun who travelled to Germany to Christianise Saxons. During the night a lot of people would retreat indoors and try umpteen amounts of ways to protect themselves from witchcraft e.g., lighting bonfires to ward off evil spirits etc.

On this night, witches were known to ride their broomsticks to a mountain and take part in devilish activities with Satan. In modern Germany, people celebrate by partying, drinking beer, eating traditional German food, dressing in costume, playing pranks and singing lots of songs. Walpurgis generally has a party atmosphere. Here are some ways you can celebrate:

- Make witchy cocktails with friends and dress up in your witchy finery. The fancier the better!
- Buy yourself crystals or gift them to others.
- Ice pentagrams onto cookies (can bake them or shop buy them).
- Have an outdoor bonfire with family and friends.
- Treat like Halfoween, but with a witchy twist e.g., watch witch films and TV shows.

I personally love this tradition! Another tradition that I had never heard of before researching for this book, but it is right up my witchy street! Let your inner witch out and have fun on this holiday!

Springoween: May (Cemetery Appreciation Month)

A lot of people find cemeteries to be scary places to be in. Who would want to wander across dead people's resting places? For me, I find them to be incredibly peaceful. I love looking at the gravestones. If you're in a particularly old graveyard then the chances are the gravestones will be over 100 years old, maybe even more. I love reading the names of all these people who lived so long ago, imagining what their lives might have been like, what their families were like, what jobs they worked as etc.

Ironically, cemeteries can also be full of life. Beautiful flowers, plants and trees can blossom all around, making everything look absolutely stunning. Cemeteries are obviously places that you can pay respects to your loved ones that have passed. It can be a great way to process death if you struggle to.

The Victorians make another appearance in this section. As I said, they were obsessed with death due to the large death count in this era. So many people were dying of either poor malnutrition, living conditions, hygiene, **actual murder** etc. They also had a lot of strange customs when burying their dead. The Victorian age was a kooky era, full of surprises, not all of them good either...

Burying the Dead

The Victorians were extremely superstitious when it came to death and the practise of burying their dead. At the time of a death, the curtains would be drawn, and the clocks would be stopped. Mirrors would be covered with material to stop the deceased person's spirit from being trapped within the glass.

Wakes could last from 2-3 days, to give people time to come and pay their respects. Flowers and candles were used to mask the disgusting odours that filled the room. During mourning periods, it was common for people to carry handkerchiefs. Most of these were black bordered, wide borders indicated a recent death.

Buried Alive

In some extreme cases, people could be accidentally buried alive. Doctors mistakenly diagnosing them to have been in a "coma" these unfortunate people would have been discovered alive in their caskets. To stop this from happening, the Victorians buried some people with a rope attached to their hand which was connected to a bell on the outside of the coffin. If the person awoke, they could ring the bell to signal help. Now this is a specific irrational fear that I now have!

Black ribbons

Another strange superstition was if several members of the same family died, people entering the home were expected to wear black ribbons, to stop the deaths from spreading. Close family members were expected to wear black during the mourning period, which was probably why Queen Victoria only wore black after she lost her beloved Prince Albert. These black ribbons were also extended to family pets, including dogs and even chickens! The Victorians were very precocious about their pets.

Bad Luck

Superstitions were rife in the Victorian era, even more than the broken mirror superstition. People believed that if you didn't cover your mouth when yawning, your spirit would leave you and the devil would enter your body. You should never wear anything new to funeral, focusing specifically on shoes.

I'm sure you know the superstition about opening an umbrella indoors is bad luck. Would you like to know why? It's particularly bizarre. They believed if you opened an umbrella indoors or drop one on the floor then a murder will happen in the house. Yes, a murder. And I thought I was paranoid!

Omens

Aside from bad luck, Victorians also believed in omens and signs that death was on the horizon, *literally*. A few of these omens include seeing an owl during the daytime then there will be a death, rain in an open grave means a family member of yours will die within a year. The smell of roses when there are no roses around means someone will die. "Everything comes in threes" coincides with if two deaths happen in a family, a third will follow. Flowers will grow on a good person's grave; weeds will grow on a bad person's grave.

Grave robbers

I'm amazed at how the Victorians were so obsessed with death but also terrified of it. It's an interesting idea that they had all of these "rules" to stop bad things happening and also took extreme measures to respect the dead. I didn't realise how many modern superstitions stem from them.

Speaking of being obsessed with death, another issue that the Victorians faced was "grave robbing". These people were known as "Resurrectionists" and were normally employed to snatch bodies used for anatomical research. They stole everything from jewellery, rings and the bodies themselves. Some people were even buried with cages over their graves, to stop these robbers from stealing their bodies.

Two infamous grave robbers were Burke and Hare. I'm proud to say that I first learnt about these from *Horrible Histories*, when Matthew Baynton played the elderly surgeon Robert Knox, the man who was swindled epically by Burke and Hare. The song that he sang told the story of how Burke and Hare tricked this surgeon, murdering innocent people and bringing them to Knox in exchange for money. Knox believed that all of these victims were friends of the pair, and because of the poor living conditions, it wasn't hard to believe that all of these people died naturally.

According to North East Nostalgic, Burke and Hare might have learnt their trade, in Sunderland! Before they moved to Edinburgh, Burke and Hare lived in Sunderland in the 1820s, and thus moving to Edinburgh to begin their horrifying trade. The Holy Trinity Church was an easy target for grave robbing. It was surrounded by sea and open land. When night fell, ghostly mists would roll in, providing perfect cover for these thieves to sneak and steal bodies as they pleased. It's wild to think that somewhere not too far from where I live was known for gruesome body snatchers.

Picnics in Purgatory

I know that I've mentioned picnics **a lot** throughout this book, but now I finally get to talk about how the Victorians had picnics in cemeteries. Again, Victorians were so fascinated by death that they wanted to be as close to it as possible, by treating cemeteries as park settings to enjoy leisurely strolls and picnics by their deceased loved ones.

Americans seemed to be the first to start this modern "trend", enjoying days such as Memorial Weekend and even Thanksgiving tucking into beef sandwiches, fruit and ginger snaps next to gravestones. They would bring their families on these jaunts, breaking bread over a grave, happy children playing in and amongst the graves, walking their pets etc. It wasn't a strange thing to do back then.

Because of the high death count, graveyards were quickly filling up and it was common for new plots of land to be turned into cemeteries, even though most Victorians buried their dead in Church Graveyards. Because of the epidemics at the time, people were terrified that these settings were essentially breeding grounds for disease and death. A change of setting was needed.

Picnic Menu

A common Victorian picnic menu consisted of a meat of some sort, mostly beef, lamb or fowl. They also indulged in fresh pies, usually pigeon or veal. Sandwiches were the perfect main to also have, with cheese, lettuce, celery, cress or salted meat fillings. A pudding was never missed out of a picnic. You would have a choice of fruit turnovers, cheesecake, jam puffs etc. And lastly to wash everything down, ginger beer, lemonade or ale were popular choices to quench one's thirst on a hot day. All of these items were carried in a sturdy basket (wicker) with an added blanket to stop grass staining one's clothes. What a disaster if that were to happen! You could definitely adapt this into a more modern picnic and even enjoy the peaceful serenity that comes in a cemetery.

Around the world

Not only did Americans enjoy picnicking with their deceased loved ones, but this trend stretches **around the world.** Of course, the most common country we've heard it from is Mexico, when they celebrate *Día De Los Muertos*.

This holiday is celebrated from 31st October to 2nd November. Families would gather together to welcome back the spirits of their loved ones, over a feast of food and drink and various celebrations. They believed that the border between the living world and the spirit world would lift, and their deceased loved ones would return to their world, to dance, drink and eat with them. As a mark of respect, the living would leave their family member's favourite foods as offerings for them, as they were technically guests in their celebrations. They would also leave offerings of candles and bright marigolds.

In the Greek village of Rizana, people would gather on the first Sunday after Easter (perfectly coinciding with Springoween!) in the cemetery in their village with fold out chairs and tables and enjoy food and drinks amongst the marble headstones. There would be a lot of food, including salad, pickles, sweets, Greek Easter eggs, and vodka! The Greeks would leave red eggs and a shot of vodka on the graves, making sure that everyone had something to eat. This tradition dates all the way back to 440 BC! I love that a small village kept up this tradition for so many years.

Another country this activity occurred in was Russia, particularly in Moscow. Moscow graveyards are wide plots of land with huge mausoleums and stunning old architecture. Russians would frequently picnic on their ancestor's graves with big baskets of food and drink. These feasts would often turn into drinking sprees and when people were banned from drinking on the streets, they would frequently retreat to graveyards to drink. If you were stopped by a policeman, you could say "We are remembering our late friend" and they would not be able to challenge it!

How to have a cemetery picnic

Early May is the time to plant your pumpkins, kids! They recommend you plant your pumpkins during early May to June. There are three things that your pumpkins need to grow: space, sunshine, plenty of food and water. You can first start your pumpkins off by sowing the seeds indoors, keeping the pots at 20C covered by a clear plastic bag until germination, when the seeds start to germinate separate the plants into pots. Once they start growing you can move the plants into bigger pots when the roots start to fill up the pots and then eventually move them outdoors when they get bigger.

I'm definitely not a gardening expert, so don't trust my advice! Seek information and advice from resourceful gardening websites and books. Pumpkins generally take about 90-120 days to grow after the seeds have been planted. Every pumpkin is different however! Places like Tesco and Asda have even released "pumpkin planting" kits, so that you don't need to seek out the seeds yourself. I would also look in garden centres for kits like this! I still remember in 2022 we bought a pumpkin planting kit, followed all of the instructions, planted the pumpkins... nothing grew. At all. We may not have done it right, but I'm definitely trying again this year! And at the end of the experience (hopefully!) you get a lovely juicy pumpkin friend!

Lemonade Day (1ˢᵗ May)

This is a simple but effective DIY. I love drinking lemonade on a warm day. If you have a skull or spooky glass, I will serve the lemonade in there. In 2022 I bought some pumpkin shaped ice cube moulds from HomeSense, so these are the perfect ice cube shapes to have! For the lemonade itself I love blackcurrant lemonade (blackcurrant squash mixed with lemonade) which makes for a devilish purple-y red coloured drink. Or I want to try pineapple lemonade (add a splash of pineapple juice to your cold lemonade) to give it an exotic flavour! Enjoy your beverage outside (the days will be getting warmer hopefully) either on a warm evening, listening to the breeze or to start your day in the morning.

National Paranormal Day (3ʳᵈ May)

Paranormal: denoting events or phenomena such as telekinesis or clairvoyance that are beyond scope of normal scientific understanding.

I went through a stage in secondary school where I was obsessed with anything paranormal, this included paranormal romances. I remember a particular book series that I read called "Paranormalcy" about a girl called Evie who works for the "International Paranormal Containment Agency" specialising in containing paranormal entities which included beings such as shape shifters, ghosts, faeries etc. This book has more of a focus on faery lore, but the series mainly discusses ghosts.

I often get the definitions of "paranormal" and "supernatural" mixed up, although they do both fall under the same umbrella I believe. National Paranormal Day itself was created in 2013, but the actual origins of it are mysterious. It seems to have been created to celebrate the spooky side of life, encouraging people to discuss their own paranormal experiences and UFO sightings.

It all depends on if you believe in such things. People believe in lots of things. The paranormal is a bit of controversial one. Is it on the same wavelength as Father Christmas, or the Tooth Fairy? I personally believe in ghosts and spirits. I've unfortunately never seen anything spooky, but I have had a "paranormal experience" of my own.

My paranormal experience

This happened when I was in college. My older sister lived about 15 minutes away from me. On this particular occasion she, my Mam and my cousin had gone away to Manchester for a few days to see Marilyn Manson. My sister however owned two bearded dragons, so she instructed me to go in the morning and night, turn their lights on and then switch them off at night. Fairly simple! I was able to go past on my way to college as the bus stop was just outside her house.

Now what I haven't mentioned is that my sister has told me in the past that a lot of bizarre occurrences happened in her house. I never really believed her, so I continued my merry way. I went into her house with the keys she had given me, I went upstairs, said hello to Falkor and Conrad and switched their lights on. I made sure they were okay and well and then I walk back downstairs and put my shoes on. I was stood just where the front door was. To my left was her sitting room door and next to it in the passageway was the stairs leading to upstairs. Directly in front of me was the kitchen door which was open. I remember so clearly looking at something up the stairs when out of the corner of my eye, something "flew" across the kitchen. I snapped my head up and looked at the kitchen. She had windows on the back wall of her kitchen, but she has actually covered them up with paper because she had "nosy neighbours". I thought for a moment it might have been a bird outside, but the windows were blocked.

One thing I can remember was whatever "flew" was big and white. Too big to be a moth or a fly. And not a piece of dust. After that I felt a horrible feeling that something did not want me to be there. I pulled my shoes on and **ran** out of the house. I flew down that path to the bus stop. The whole experience confused me. Had I seen a ghost? Was it a spirit or a demon? Could it have been an angel? I couldn't shake the feeling that I felt when I was standing in the passageway. Something didn't want me to be there at all. Thankfully I left before whatever it was tried other ways to get me out of the house. Don't worry, I didn't need telling twice! I always class it as a "paranormal experience" because to this day, I can't explain what I saw.

Paranormal within my family

I feel like so many families have their own ghost stories and paranormal experiences. Usually, it happens after a relative has passed away. A lot of young children claim to have spoken to the spirits of deceased family members or "played" with them. I've heard a lot of stories of them speaking to dead soldiers that either lived in their house previously or were killed on the grounds of where the house was built.

I don't remember ever seeing any ghosts as a child. I have heard a few stories from my parents though. Both say that they saw the spirits of their parents (my grandparents) after they had passed away. It wasn't a dangerous experience. More like their parents were "checking in" with them and reassuring them that they were fine.

We also owned cats throughout my whole childhood. The three that I owned growing up were named Tiger, Duke and Gizmo but my parents owned another cat that died before I was born named George. It is a well-known fact that cats can see things that humans can't. In my parent's old flat they had a mirror on the wall that belonged to my grandma. It had been in the family for generations. One evening my parents were watching the TV as normal when one of their cats suddenly started watching something that was "going across the room". There was nothing there, but it looked like the cat was watching someone walk past before leaving the room. Later on, my Mam found the mirror that had previously been hanging on the wall was now lying face up halfway across the floor. Which was strange, because you would think if it fell off the wall, gravity would pull it so it was face down unless it had flipped around. What was also strange was that it seemed like nothing had knocked it over or off the wall. So, was it a coincidence? A paranormal experience? I'm not entirely sure...

My Mam actually has quite a few ghost stories from her childhood. Whether or not they were actual whispers of people long gone coming back through the veil... you decide! When my Mam was 5 years old she has a particularly bad case of chicken pox, to the point where she hallucinated seeing her Granda George, who she had never seen or met, as he was killed by a drunk driver years beforehand, walk into her room and said to her, "You'll be okay hinny". Another story included her cousin Jim who lived with my Mam's family at the time, had a broken leg and experienced the sensation of someone getting into bed with him, when there was no one there... Even my Granda had his own paranormal experience. He was just getting dressed one day when he heard someone say the name "Jenny" even though he was by himself in the house and saw someone walk past him in the mirror. He immediately went looking for his sister whose name was Jenny in case it was a sign to check on her, but sadly not. His next-door neighbour, Jenny's husband was killed in an accident. So maybe, this was her husband asking my Granda to check on her? Either way, it's very spooky...

Grandma Annie Means

The reason that I called myself "Apple-bobbing Annie" is because of my dear Grandma, Annie Means. Although she actually hated the name Annie and went by "Nancy" for the majority of her life. My Mam gave me the middle name Annie, so I carry that piece of her with me always. It wasn't until I started writing this book that I discovered just how alike me, and my grandma were in terms of being obsessed with the paranormal. My grandma actually loved the paranormal as well and would regularly go to spiritual (or "spuggy" as she called it) meetings in Byker, although she went with her auntie and friend because she was too afraid to go by herself. She also always tried with Halloween, carving turnips, and decorating the house. I love that my grandma was so fascinated by the paranormal, just like I am.

Haunting History:

Annie Fairlamb Mellon

Another Annie that was involved with the paranormal was Annie Fairlamb Mellon, Newcastle's first Geordie medium! There isn't much online or recorded about her, so this piece of history took a lot of digging to find information on. Annie Fairlamb Mellon, also known as Mrs J.B Mellon (don't know where the J came from…) was born in Newcastle upon Tyne in 1856. At age 9 she saw apparitions of her brother being lost at sea, and by the time she reached her teen years, her interest in spiritualism was growing and growing. In 1873, Annie and another medium were employed as official mediums for the Newcastle Spiritual Evidence Society in Jesmond (which I've walked past before!).

As prolific as she was during her career, unfortunately Annie was "exposed" as a fraud in 1894. At this point she had actually relocated to Sydney; Australia and it was during a materialisation séance that she was "exposed". It seemed like there wasn't a lot of evidence into her exposure. Just here say really! Apart from the controversy, she did do private seances before her husband's death in 1896. She had relocated back to Newcastle and was able to settle into Newcastle life once again. She ended up remarrying, to the President of the Newcastle Society, Henry Gleave.

Annie died at the age of 82 in 1939 and was privately cremated. It makes me sad that a medium who was so involved in the paranormal community was "exposed" and ridiculed. The article that I used for research said at the end *"Annie's story will be told as it always should have been unbiased, thorough and kind."* And I agree whole-heartedly. Annie was just a woman who believed in creating bonds with the spirit world. I believe that I didn't really explain it well enough, but if you get a chance, research, and keep Annie in your memories. From one Annie to another...

Paranormal Media

The many portrayals of paranormal exploration in TV and film are one of my favourite forms of media. There's something about the old-school TV shows from the late 90s-early 2000s has such a sense of nostalgia for me. Now I know I mentioned about the definitions of "supernatural" and "paranormal" being mixed up, I will ironically include a TV show called "Supernatural" in this section. It does include supernatural creatures like vampires, werewolves etc but demons and ghosts are also things that are always hunted.

Dads on a hunting trip...

"Carry on my wayward son, there'll be peace when you are done, lay your weary head to rest, don't you cry no more."

Kansas – Carry On Wayward Son (1976)

The song is alone is extremely nostalgic to me! My sister first got me into watching *Supernatural* back in the day. I would also watch it with my cousin at her house on sleepovers. Back then I have to say I was a huge scaredy cat, so there were certain episodes that I would completely avoid.

One episode told the tale of Bloody Mary, you know who I'm talking about. Say her name three times and she'll appear in the mirror? I unfortunately believed in that as much as I believed in online Ouija board games and Facebook chain mail messages "if you don't pass this on, Helga will appear in your room at 12pm!". It was 2013 and I was extremely gullible okay. The internet was an interesting place back then. Back to Bloody Mary! I watched that episode at my cousin's house and it **traumatised** me. To the point where I refused to look in any mirrors! Of course, now I am older and slightly wiser, so I don't believe in silly games like that.

Before the Bloody Mary episode, we had the one that started it all, with the iconic line "Dad's on a hunting trip and hasn't been home in a few days". "Supernatural" told the story of brothers Sam and Dean, whose dad goes missing on a demon hunting trip and wants them to continue the "family business". The show had everything; action, supernatural/paranormal lore, romance, drama, and it tugs, no, it **rips** your heart strings out. Not to mention the two lead actors are **incredibly attractive**! I was always a "Sam girl" but now I appreciate just how rugged Dean is!

Ghost Whisperer "Pilot" review:

I decided to watch the first episode of another paranormal TV show called *Ghost Whisperer* to get a feel for other TV shows. So, here is the review!

The episode had a bit of a slow build up to the story/world building. It had an interesting concept, and it reminded me of a book I read when I was younger (couldn't tell you the name of the book!). It must be hard for the main character because she's treated as both the villain and the hero (and this is only in the first episode!). I also love the setting of the small town, it gave me major *Gilmore Girls* (ultimate autumnal show!) vibes, as well as the setting of the antique shop.

The Haunted Collector

I used to watch a TV show with my Mam when I was younger called *The Haunted Collector*. About a man named Mr John Zaffis (amazing name) who travels across America with a team of investigators, visiting various haunted locations. He usually looks specifically for objects that have spirits attached or trigger paranormal activity, which he then takes at the end of the programme and places in his 'museum'.

The fact that he owns a "paranormal artifacts museum" is already so cool. I forgot to mention that the team of investigators are also made up of members of his family. I told you ghost-hunting was fun for all the family! The show ran for 3 seasons, from 2011 to 2013 on Syfy. I remember it being a bit of a "filler show", something to watch on an afternoon, but I genuinely loved it, it was so bad that it was good!

World Bee Day (20th May)

These fuzzy little superheroes are **so** important and really are the saviours of our eco-system! World Bee Day's aim is to raise awareness of the ways that we can protect and save the bees. Bees are incredibly important, and we don't even know why. When I was younger, I was always a little frightened of bees. I didn't really like any insect with wings, even if a butterfly fluttered in my direction I would scream and run in the other direction! It's crucial to especially teach children that bees aren't something to be frightened of, which is why I'm including some fun bee facts here and tips on how to help the bees!

Bee facts:

- Bees do a "waggle dance" which is a way for them to communicate with other bees on where to find the best sources for food. This dance took 2 years to decode by Sussex University!
- Bees actually have 4 wings! 2 of their wings hook together to make a larger pair, and then they unhook when they're not flying.
- 1 out of 3 mouthfuls of our food depends on bee pollinators! They really are busy little folk!

- Bees have "smelly footprints" that distinguish between themselves, relatives and strangers. This was researched by the University of Bristol.
- Bees can't actually see the colour red, if they land on red flowers, it's because they can see the UV patterns that are in flowers!

How to help the bees:

- Plant traditional cottage flowers such as primrose, lavender, foxglove and marigolds. Bees can't get enough of them!
- If you see a struggling bee friend on the ground, give them a little energy boost by mixing half and half white sugar and water on a teaspoon or upturned drinks cap. Place it in a sheltered area for them to refresh themselves.
- Avoid pesticides and herbicides when you're gardening. Always allow "weeds" to grow to feed the bees. Dandelions are a great source of food for bees in early spring. Don't cut or pick them!
- Make a "bee bath" for your fuzzy friends. Fill a shallow bowl or bird bath with clean water, add pebbles and stones for them to break the water's surface to keep themselves hydrated!
- Grow fruit trees; strawberries, cherries, raspberries in particular are tasty for you and the bees!

Spread the sweet message!

Have a "boo-bee" picnic/party/fundraiser! Channel Eugene and Wednesday in *Wednesday* and become a gothic beekeeper! If you're a particularly charitable human who enjoys getting involved in your local community, you could have a bee-themed fundraiser. Make leaflets with bee information for people to read. Sell locally-made honey, bee-themed artworks and trinkets, sweet treats (honeycomb chocolate, boo-bee cupcakes, etc!) to spread the honey-sweet messages of bees.

If this isn't your style, you could do something more low-key. Yes, I'm talking about **picnics!** Plant some flowers and seeds in your garden, make your bee bath so you can snack, and they can have a drink too! Eat your bee-themed sweet treats. You could draw your own boo-bees if you're particularly artistic or look for some colouring sheets. Colouring in is so therapeutic! The more people know about bees, the better, and you're doing it in style! Boo-bees are adorable.

World Goth Day (22nd May)

Goth Day originally began in May 2009, when a British radio station was discussing different music subcultures. From this little discussion, Goth music DJs "Cruel Britannia" and Martin Oldgoth created "World Goth Day". The day falls on the 22nd May every year and celebrates the culture of Goth. There are so many different subcultures within Goth!

The Gothic culture itself can be tracked back to the 1980s, but I feel like it goes back even further. You could say that Queen Victoria was the original Goth, as she wore black every day for the rest of her life after her husband, Prince Albert sadly died. Some of the subcultures of goth are goth rock, goth metal, steampunk, dark cabaret, dark wave, cold wave, gothabilly etc. There's so many to choose from!

Goths, a lot of the time, are misunderstood. They are seen as moody, loners, weird etc. Just because they enjoy outwardly expressing their fashion and music style! When I was in secondary school, I hung out with the "emo's" and Goths. They were the nicest group of people I had ever met! They loved media such as Twilight, bands like Fall Out Boy and Paramore, they read vampire books and weren't afraid to be themselves. I was particularly close to three girls and one boy within that group who I still remember fondly to this day, despite losing touch over the years due to adulthood.

Something I remember them doing in particular was making roleplaying Facebook profiles with characters that they had created, with inspiration took from *Twilight*. I was all about that! I was still wrapping my brain around the *Twilight* hype, but creating your own characters and storylines? The wannabe author in me was **squealing**. I wanted to play along so badly, but even then, I felt like I wasn't cool enough!

I remember one of the girls had actually created her own story and a cast of characters. She had written about 3 sisters who were also emo/Goth, with family who also divulged in the Gothic lifestyle and a group of friends who were in the emo/Goth crowd. These friends had two bands; one I think was named "Static Heart"? That featured the three sisters in it also. I remember loving reading all of the characters profiles that she had written. The characters became so real to me. She actually, **incredibly kindly**, gave me the characters and said I could write the story if I wanted. I still have all of the notes and profiles tucked in a notebook somewhere. Who knows, I might dig the Hale family back out for their own debut! I have her to thank for them!

Because of my Goth friends, I definitely embody a little touch of Goth in my everyday style. I obviously absolutely love Halloween, black is definitely my favourite colour to wear, I get a bit giddy if I see a skull, I love Tim Burton films, I am still a hardcore listener of Fall Out Boy and Panic at the Disco (and rock music) and I've always wanted to be like Wednesday Addams. Yes, I also love pink and Disney films, but you don't have to squeeze yourself into one box! The beauty of being a Goth is to be anything you like.

How to celebrate Goth culture

Here's some ways you can celebrate Goth culture. Remember, there's no right or wrong way of celebrating but here's some ideas that I thought sounded fun!

- Watch Gothic films and TV shows. You could have a Tim Burton marathon, Twilight marathon, watch all of the old Universal Classic Monster films, the Addams Family TV show and films etc. Anything that oozes Goth energy is a must!

- Read Gothic literature. Books such as Dracula, The Woman in Black, Wuthering Heights, The Picture of Dorian Gray etc. There are also plenty of modern books that have Gothic vibes, and quite a few "reimagining's" and retellings of classic Gothic literature. Gothic or Dark Academia is a genre that is becoming a lot more popular nowadays, you could explore and read.

- Wear your darkest outfit. The blacker the better! Paint your nails black, do a dark smoky eye, extravagant eyeliner etc. You don't have to wear a particular style of Goth, but then you don't have to be just one! Dip into all the subgenres if you like.

- Listen to Goth music. Think artists such as Siouxsie and the Banshees, The Cure, Depeche Mode, The Skeletal Family (whose name was taken from a David Bowie song!), Sisters of Mercy etc.

- Donate to the Sophie Lancaster Foundation. This is an incredibly sad case that never should have happened, but thankfully the foundation is doing amazing work spreading awareness.

- Shop from Gothic small businesses. I personally love buying from small shops (as I've mentioned before) and there are many small shops that are Gothic themed! *Simply Gothic* produces Gothic jewellery, stationery and home décor.

The Sophie Lancaster Foundation

As I mentioned earlier, Goths are often misunderstood, and people judge them for being "different". I talked about my Goth friends before, but what I didn't mention then was that they also unfortunately were bullied and judged for standing out from the crowd. There were so many times that they were treated wrongly, by their own peers, and teachers never did a thing about it. My heart hurt for them. Thankfully in later years my school pushed a zero-tolerance on bullying rule. But sometimes, it's too little too late.

I want to discuss the Sophie Lancaster case, which occurred on 11th August 2007. I won't go into too many details about the case; I will just talk about the basic facts. Sophie was a young woman who lived her life as a Goth. She and her boyfriend were both lovely, creative people just living their lives. That all ended on that fateful day in August, they were walking through a park when they were attacked by 5 boys who called them names like "freak, mosher, weirdo". Unfortunately, Sophie did not survive the attack and passed away in the hospital at the age of 20 years old, after being in hospital on life support for 13 days.

Her whole life was yanked away from her, because she dressed differently to others. The case impacted so many people, whether you were a Goth or not. The Sophie Lancaster Foundation was set up in honour of the legacy that she left behind. The Foundation aims to stamp out prejudice and image-based hate crimes forever. Since the charity has been set up there have been events, documentaries, a BBC film, festivals, a theatrical play and so much more. They have a website which chronicles all of the charity's progress, gives information about how to support, there's even a page where you can buy merch to support the cause. The charity also goes into schools to educate children on equality and diversity and respect of different communities. So, if you do anything this World Goth Day, support the Sophie Lancaster Foundation in any way you can, I'm sure it would make Sophie and her Mum smile.

www.sophielancasterfoundation.com

Whitby Goth Weekend (28th-30th April)

Another activity that you could do on World Goth Day is visit Whitby for their annual Goth Weekend! The Whitby Goth weekend was founded in 1994 by Jo Hampshire, and it is an alternative music event that celebrates Goth culture. It happens every spring and autumn and attracts thousands of visits! It isn't just about music though. Everyone comes dressed up in their best Gothic finery. There's also a huge market which has so many stalls selling Goth jewellery, artwork, trinkets etc. It really is the best celebration for Goth culture!

Since I'm from England I always used to think that Britain didn't have much to offer on the Halloween front. We just get our Halloween season in October and that's it. But through research I've discovered that we actually have quite a lot of spooky culture in the UK! America obviously goes all out all year around, but thankfully the UK is catching up! If you have the time and the means to travel to this event I highly recommend it! It's on my bucket list to travel there, and it's in England and I want to promote more spooky events in my home country!

Whitby is also a beautiful little coastal town, framed by soft sands and frothy blue sea. So not only are you in an area surrounded by Goths and the most interesting people in exquisite outfits and costumes, but it has a fabulous backdrop! There's lots of cafes and restaurants that you can visit for lunch, and also classic chippies! If you're not a Brit, a "chippy" is our name for a fish and chip shop. It's practically criminal to not get fish and chips when you go to the seaside! The smell of vinegar, the salty chips, mushy peas... just watch out for those pesky seagulls! They're like flying vampires themselves, thirsting for vinegary battered cod!

125 Years of Dracula (2022)

Whitby, you sly spooky devil! I didn't realise that Whitby had even more spooky heritage, being the birthplace of Bram Stoker's Dracula. Dracula was originally published in 1897 as Bram Stoker arrived in Whitby and was apparently inspired by the dramatic headlands and abbey ruins to write *Dracula*. To think that Bram Stoker himself was inspired by a small, seaside town to write one of the most iconic spooky books in history is so inspiring. Everyone knows Dracula, it's been adapted over a hundred times, it's inspired so many films and TV shows, fashion styles etc. Even things like *Twilight* or *The Vampire Diaries* wouldn't exist without the influence of Dracula!

2022 marked the 125th anniversary of Dracula and to celebrate they had a **huge** event. This event actually was awarded a World Record for the largest gathering of people dressed as vampires! The Whitby Abbey was illuminated with a projection of bats to also mark the occasion. The sun was definitely shining down on this fang-tastic event! I would be in absolute awe if I saw that happen. Bring a copy of *Dracula* to grab a photo in front of the ruins, you couldn't get a better picture than that! You could even turn visiting Whitby into a road trip event! Start at the top of the country in Edinburgh, visit the Frankenstein Bar and then work your way down the country until you meet Dracula in Whitby!

I think this might be the best thing I've ever heard! Being surrounded by people dressed in the best vampire costumes, having fun being creepy and kooky. I unfortunately could not find the time to go to this weekend, but I still think you can celebrate Dracula and all things gothic in your own way! As I always say, you can celebrate in whatever way you like, but these are some small ideas that you can do!

- Watch Dracula or any adaptation of Dracula (my favourite is *Dracula: Dead and Loving it*, it's pure camp!).
- Read Dracula, Dracula retellings or any vampire book (*The Reluctant Vampire Queen* by Jo Simmons is a light and funny YA vampire book that I particularly loved!).
- Wear a vampire costume around the house. You could even do this with friends and family and gather everyone around for a blood bash!
- Drink some blood… only joking! Although cranberry juice looks very similar…

Stranger Things 4 release (27th May 2022)

Of all the TV shows that I've ever watched, *Stranger Things* has always stuck with me. When I was a child, I loved films such as *The Goonies, Hocus Pocus, Casper, Labyrinth, Honey I Shrunk the Kids, Peter Pan* (the 2003 version!) etc. Children's fantasy films that followed groups of children on an adventure, either facing a great evil or tumbling into a mystical land.

When I was a late teen I developed a love for 80s films and the actor River Phoenix. That corresponded into the films that I began to discover e.g.,. *Stand By Me, The Lost Boys, The Monster Squad, Return to Oz, Teen Wolf* etc. A lot of these were teenagers facing off against a great evil. *Stand By Me* was my favourite film for years. Based on a novella written by Stephen King, it was about 4 boys who go on a search to find the missing body of a local boy. It didn't exactly have any fantasy elements, but it still had the "adventure" aspect, with a grim outcome!

Stranger Things embodies everything that I've spoken about here! It has the core group dynamic, they're up against supernatural monsters, it's set in the 1980s with plenty of pop culture references and nostalgia, it's creepy and eerie! Ever since the show was released, it's paved a path for other shows and films with a similar style, my favourites being *Super 8,* about a group of teens making a short film who witness an alien landing, and the reboot of *IT* (again by Stephen King) now set in the 1980s rather than the 1950s like in the miniseries.

On the 27th of May 2022, we saw the release of Season 4, which brings the story now to high school, the once baby-faced kids now being angsty teenagers. I have to say, I think Season 4 is my favourite season by far! There was something about how it was more elevated, we had new characters and higher stakes. To me, each season reminded me of a different 80s film, let's list them, shall we!

- Season 1 (**Stand by Me**). As I've said, *Stand by Me*, was my favourite 80s film when I was a teenager. I watched it so many times that I could recite the script backwards! Season 1 had a comforting feeling like when I watched the film. The kids were practically babies who enjoyed playing DnD in Mike's basement. Then Will goes missing and they have to "search" for Will. Weirdly, there is actually an episode called "The Body" which is what the original novella was called. There are a few scenes that mirror the film, where the core four are walking along the train tracks, just like our kids from Castle Rock walked down.
- Season 2 (**The Monster Squad/The Goonies**) I like to call this the 'pumpkin spice' season! The first few episodes are based around Halloween, so we get to see a lot of 1980s Halloween with some pop culture costumes (the boys as Ghostbusters, Max as Michael Myers!). I like to call this the 'Halloween Special' of Stranger Things. The autumnal background, the cosy knitwear, the Halloween scenes etc. The kids were now the same age as the Goonies e.g., 12-13, they were still on that adventure-mystery narrative, but spooky! Mike was still pining for Eleven, Dustin made a new creature friend, new girl Max started at their school, lots of turmoil happening!

- Season 3 (**The Lost Boys**) The Hawkins kids are now teenagers, not too old but still growing up fast! It's the height of summer, the sun is hot and there's a new mall opening in the sleepy little town. The kids aren't into playing DnD in Mike's basement anymore (much to Will's annoyance!). They're a lot like the teenagers in *The Lost Boys*. They're enjoying the summer when a new threat comes to town. They've had 3 seasons worth of threats though so now at least they're a bit more equipped to deal with it!
- Season 4 (**Nightmare on Elm Street**) This season now takes a horror film angle. Vecna very much reminds me of Freddy Krueger, the way he invades your mind and puts you into a dream-like state. Especially the scenes in the first few episodes I was terrified! The monsters in the first few seasons just seemed creepy to me, but now they were genuinely **scary**. The kids are also now older teenagers, to go with the audience of teen horror/slashers. They're dealing with popularity groups, high school clubs, dating, high school sports, mental health, new friendships etc. It's also nice to see the kids grow up from adorable kids to young adults.

Premiere Pizza Party!

I was very hyped up for the first episode of Season 4. From the trailers, the season posters, it felt like it took ages to come out! It was so worth it though when I watched it. We got a lot of new characters this season, one of them is particular was Argyle, Jonathon's friend in California. Argyle is a typical Californian "stoner", who works for *Surfer Boy Pizza*. We get a few pizza scenes and one epic scene of Argyle making a ham and pineapple pizza "Try before you deny!".

If you were planning on having a premiere party or since by now it's already came out, you could have a pizza party to watch the season with your friends. Either order in, make your own or buy frozen pizzas. You could have a buffet of different toppings and swap around flavours. You could also do a feast of other Stranger Things-themed foods or even 80s themed snacks! Could channel Season 3 vibes with some Scoops Ahoy themed ice-cream! I love having a themed feast, as you can tell by the number of picnics I've included in this book!

Make some Stranger Things décor; Joyce's fairy lights bunting, include actual fairy lights or you could have a activity going on while you watch the show, if you're good at multi-tasking! *Stranger Things* really gives you the most immersive experience. There are so many themed board games out there that you could play. Even DnD! Play DnD with Season 4 on in the background, how meta!

Travel back to the 1980s...

To celebrate and reminisce about the release of Season 4, I decided to read *Stranger Things*-esque books throughout May! I love preparing themed reads in certain months, this month's reads were particularly exciting to read! I looked far and wide for books that reminds me of the show or simply gave off similar vibes. Now, let's time travel back to the 80s with some gnarly book reviews!

National Biscuit Day (29th May)

What do you dip in your cuppa? For me, I love a good biscuit. Custard creams, chocolate digestives, bourbons etc. I'm really not fussy! This Halloween hack is very simple. Pick your best Halloween mug with your favourite hot drink whether that's a milky brew, a hot chocolate, coffee etc. If you have a spooky plate, or crockery, I would use that and then choose your biscuit selection, whether you choose a few different biscuits or a plate of the same. If you enjoy baking, you could even make your own biscuits (spiced pumpkin cookies anyone?). You could decorate some biscuits to make them spooky e.g., turn Oreos into spiders! The possibilities are endless!

Summerween

June to August

Dear Summerween,

Creep-a-bunga, my dudes! I have never been so happy to see your sunny smile! Springoween is blooming into a brighter flower, a cheerful yellow flower that looks like the sun. The days are getting warmer; dandelions and

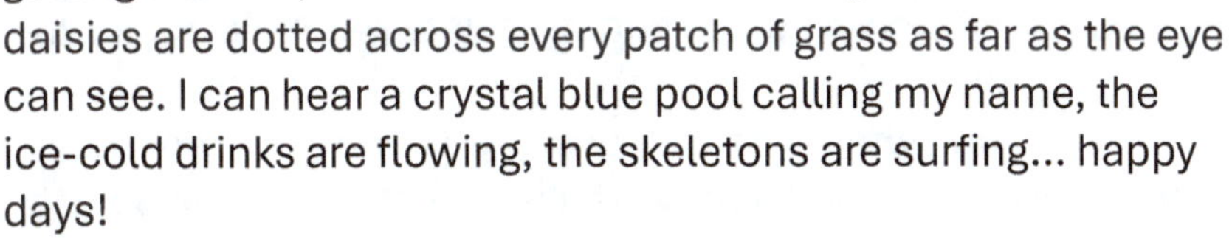

daisies are dotted across every patch of grass as far as the eye can see. I can hear a crystal blue pool calling my name, the ice-cold drinks are flowing, the skeletons are surfing... happy days!

Summerween is Jack-o-Melons, ghosts floating on inflatable rings, skeletons in sunglasses, sea witches casting beachy magic... I have to say, Summerween might be my favourite season! The sun makes everyone happy. As soon as the weather gets a little bit warmer and the days become a little bit brighter in the UK, us Brits are straight down the beach, in the garden, setting up the barbeques, Mams making "picky teas", the paddling pools are out to cool your feet in, we love the hot weather! We don't get much of it to be honest, so you have to treasure every sunray!

As I said, we like to visit our seaside coasts as much as possible in the summer. I love the seaside; I have so many happy memories of being at the seaside with my family. We used to visit one particular coast a lot, called Cullercoats. Whenever my parents would buy a new car, we would 'christen' it by buying fish and chips and eating them in the car. Even then my order was a battered sausage, chips and lots of batter! Fish and chips really are a British delicacy, enjoyed only by sitting on the warm sand with the sun shining!

I've also discovered some gorgeous beaches with my cousins. My younger cousin lives in a small village, and they love to take their dogs on beach walks. On one particular day when I was staying over and we had gone out for the day; we found a little chippy and I decided to switch up my order after listening to recommendations and decided to go for cheesy chips and gravy. It was truly life changing. *Try before you deny!*

Another reason why I love the seaside is the hidden treasures. When I was little, I would fill my pockets up with seashells, stones, seaweed, anything I could find (much to the dismay of my Mam!). I was so drawn to finding found materials, shells in particular. I was always looking for the prettiest or the most unusual looking shells to take home. I still carry this wonder with me into adulthood. I never realised that it was basically beach magic until now! Maybe I was a sea witch all along...

A couple of years ago I visited a little coastal village called Amble. The beach was little and almost hidden, small and sweet. I was looking for beach materials like I always do when I discovered the tiny shell of a crab! It was a little bit bigger than my thumb, a golden-brown colour. I was amazed! I had never found anything so interesting. This little creature in my hand had lived and breathed in the ocean, seeing things humans could only dream of seeing! From then on, I really wanted to find more, I did end up finding some more crab shells in different sizes, they've been added to my collection!

On the flipside of Summerween, apart from beach magic, I also love funfairs! Fairgrounds, ghost trains, helter skelters, *"scream if you want to go faster!"* and pink candyfloss. Every June in Newcastle, a travelling funfair comes to town. It's called 'The Hoppings' and it pitches up at the Town Moor. It goes on for a week and a bit and I remember going every summer as a child. The smell of hot dogs and onions, the sound of the Magic Mouse ride, feeling scared walking past the ghost train, *"are you on going on the bungee?"* and buying a massive sugar dummy at an overpriced stall are all vivid

Hoppings memories! The spooky side of the Hoppings is that it's **cursed**! Legend has it the funfair was cursed by an elderly gypsy woman, who was angry that she was kicked out of the fair, so she cursed the fairground with a plague of rain. Without fail, every year it always rains! Whether or not the legend is actually true is another story, it still always rains!

Summerween is also when my birthday is! I was born on the 17th of August, ironically, in a thunderstorm! I was always very lucky that my birthday fell in the summer holidays, I was able to celebrate in the glorious sunshine! I was actually one of the youngest in my year group, so I would go to school at the end of term with a traybake and a cardboard birthday badge saying it was "Nearly My Birthday"! It was fun to celebrate with my school friends before my actual birthday. I love making my birthday spooky now! For my 25th my family very kindly held a Halloween-themed 'party tea' for me, with *Hocus Pocus* in the background! It was a very special day.

Feel free to step into the freezing cold waters of Summerween. Imagine a Halloween-themed beach club... that's what Summerween is! We have monster burgers, pumpkin pineapple cocktails, ice-cream skulls, Frankenstein's Monster is the DJ, blasting out tunes like *Monster Mash* and *The Purple People Eater*. Dracula is handing out "blood shots" (*approach with caution*!). There are sirens mysteriously dragging men off into the deep end of the pool... it's all happening at **Halloween Havana**! Come on in, the water's fine!

National Fish and Chip Day (2nd June)

"Oh, I do like to be beside the seaside, oh I do like to be beside the sea. Oh, I do like to stroll along the prom, prom, prom where the brass bands play. Tiddley-om-pom-pom!"

John H. Glover-Kind: I Do Like to Be Beside the Seaside.

Sea, sand, fish and chips really goes hand in hand together! You can't not visit a beach without buying a portion of cod and chips, coating it in obscene amounts of salt and vinegar and sitting on the warm sands, shielding your meal as seagulls try to divebomb you for a cheeky chip. Contrary to popular belief, fish and chips was not actually invented in England, but actually originated from 15th century Poland, and the first 'takeaway' fish and chip shop opened in East London, in 1860.

Hungry History

"Four bags of chips then... and I want 12 chicken nuggets, a small battered hot dog, plenty of onions, plenty of sauce... Get a move on, that chippy, it's every man for himself on a Friday night!"- Derry Girls.

Yes, this is **hungry**, not **haunting history**! According to North East Nostalgic, fish and chips were a popular favourite in Edwardian times. They used to be fried in beef dripping on coal fired ranges. They were known as the "working class supper", a cheap and filling meal that was provided for 'pit people'. No such thing as 'posh' cardboard boxes then; in those days they came wrapped up in newspaper! Chippies were even known as meeting places for courting couples, as pubs had not welcomed women yet! My parents often frequented Cullercoats chippy on 'dates' before introducing its delights to my sisters and I when we were kids.

Later on, Fish and chips were the only meal that was not rationed during World War II. The government of the time believed that keeping this comfort meal would boost the morale of the people. Nowadays, chippies are more common in towns, although kebab and pizza shops are becoming more popular takeaways. However, there's nothing quite like driving to the coast on a warm day and popping to a chippy!

Salt & Vinegar 'Summer Slasher' date!

Yes, thank you, that title is one of my favourites! For National Fish and Chip Day, or any day during Summerween really, I think it would be a great idea to take yourself on a solo date to the coast. Wear your favourite Summerween outfit, take a Gothic parasol if you want! Grab some fish and chips for lunch. Find a comfortable spot, either on the beach, near some rocks, or even on the pier (if there is one).

My favourite kind of solo dates are bookish dates. I love reading in spots other than my bedroom. For this date I would bring a 'summer slasher' book with you. Summer horror books are also acceptable for this! If you can't find a horror that's has summer vibes you can always just bring any horror that takes your fancy. While you're indulging in your salty chips, you can flick through your book, getting lost in a scary world while the sun shines on your face!

National Cheese Day (4th June)

I am a cheese lover. Cheddar, mozzarella, brie, camembert, any kind of cheese - I love it! At **Ghoulia Childs** [@ghouliachilds]; they make spooky food designs! They shared a post for National Cheese Day with a "cheese graveyard" board. I love a cheese/charcuterie board. You can add any sides you want, and any type of cheese! This isn't my original idea, but I wanted to share it because I think it would be super cool to make!

How to make:

- Coffin shaped brie. Take a brie circle and turn it into a coffin! You can either slice it up yourself or use a coffin cutter. Make it the centrepiece of the board.

- Tombstone cheese cubes. Use cross tombstone as the inspiration for this one. The cheese used for this looks like Red Leicester.
- Gravestone slices. Use flat cheese slices (can be any you want, on the photo they are stood up, but you can have them lying down if you want! Use a cutter or your own steady hand for this.
- Skull ham. I feel like ham goes perfectly on a cheese board. Whether it's fancy ham or supermarket ham, you could use a skull cutter to make some skulls for the board, to add to the gothic vibes.
- Scary sides. Anything else you'd like to add? Go for things like olives, pickles, grapes, crackers, a dip or chutney if you want some spread for your crackers.
- Halloween décor. You can add any other small pieces of décor to fit around your food, e.g., mini pumpkins, mini skulls etc.

World Bike Day (4th June)

Fun fact: I can't ride a bike! I had no balance throughout my childhood so learning to ride a bike was quite hard for me! I didn't want to deny anyone else of their bicycle experience though! I was actually inspired by a TikTok (@maplegrace_) for this activity!

The TikTok was captioned "Random bike rides & the ST soundtrack". In the video they packed a bag with a sketchbook, chalks, and headphones and went off on a bike ride in the countryside with the *Stranger Things* soundtrack playing in their headphones. It seemed like such a chilled activity. Heading outdoors with minimal items and great music is a perfect thing to do on a summer's day!

You can change this in whatever way you like. You could change the destination, the route, you could take a picnic with you to have at your destination and entertainment e.g., a colouring book, your current read etc. Let yourself get lost in the music from *Stranger Things* and reminisce about your favourite moments from the series!

Cornetto Trilogy weekend! (3rd June-4th June 2022)

"Do you want anything from the shop?" "Cornetto."- Shaun of the Dead.

Having a themed movie marathon is **such** a fun thing to do! In my Winterween letter I explained that I watched the film *Shaun of the Dead* for the first time in 2021. I was obsessed and I watched it every day during winter. I then decided to explore the rest of the trilogy, the "Cornetto trilogy"! It's a series of films starring two main actors (Simon Pegg and Nick Frost) and a cast of recurring actors. Each film may have different storylines, but it always mentions Cornetto ice-creams. The trilogy is thus known as the "Three Flavours" trilogy!

In June 2022, me and my cousins decided to celebrate one of my cousins moving into her first flat with a movie marathon weekend. We of course decided on watching the *Cornetto Trilogy*, with authentic Cornetto ice-creams! I was picked up around 3 by my cousin and then we went to pick up our other cousin and travel back to the new flat. We started the weekend on the Friday night and finished watching the films on Saturday night.

Friday: We started off the night by having a Domino's takeaway pizza for tea (classic movie night food!). I chose the cheeseburger pizza and potato wedges (superb choice!), and we stuck on *Hot Fuzz* for our first film. I had never seen it before then as I was waiting until the marathon to watch it. I did enjoy *Hot Fuzz*; it may not have been my favourite of the trilogy, but it was an enjoyable watch! *Still Game* with scary cult vibes!

Also, while we watched the film, we played a board game I got for my birthday which was called "Stupid Deaths" *it's funny cause they're true!*. This was a perfect spooky game that you could also play at Halloween! Guessing stupid deaths throughout history while running away from the Grim Reaper. After we played the game, we had a few drinks and finished the film, but the rest of the night is a bit hazy to me....

Saturday: We woke up, had breakfast and decided to head out for the day. Obviously, if you're thinking of recreating this movie marathon you don't have to do this part, but we decided to head out for some fresh air. We popped over to Asda and grabbed some bits for, you've guessed it, a picnic! Drinking game: down a shot every time I mention picnics in this book!

After our food shop we decided to go to Jesmond Dene. If you're not from Newcastle, Jesmond Dene is a historic natural park in the middle of the city. It has a forest, a waterfall, old mill ruins and "Pet's Corner" where you can see different animals. I love Jesmond Dene. I spent a lot of time there as a child. It's scenic, peaceful and very calming. We found a nice, shaded spot to have our picnic and then took a walk through the forest and around.

On the journey back to my cousin's flat we got some takeaway drinks from Costa and then began the last leg of the marathon! We went in order with *Shaun of the Dead* and finishing with *The World's End*. We also then whipped out the Cornetto's as our movie snack! I'll say it once and I'll say it again. I love *Shaun of the Dead*! We finished off the night with more drinks and a picky tea.

In the words of the greatest character in the Cornetto Trilogy: *"Me, they call me the King..."*. I have to say, the first time I watched *The World's End* I wasn't a huge fan. But it was definitely the character Gary King that pulled me in. If you are wanting to have a Cornetto Trilogy weekend, you could try a pub crawl like Gary and the lads. You could adapt this marathon in any way you like! I enjoyed doing a mix of activities, chill and active!

Sea-Glass Hunting at Seaham Beach

This happened during Springoween, but I had a lovely day at the beach with my sister and my niece, hunting for sea glass! The beach we went to was Seaham Beach in Sunderland, which is apparently "famous" for finding beautiful pieces of sea glass. Sea glass, in general, absolutely fascinates me! Little pieces of man-made glass washed up into the sea and transformed into beautiful little gems!

The beach itself was stunning. It had stony parts where there were the possibilities of finding sea glass, but you had to look extremely carefully otherwise you would miss them altogether! We also came across an ethereal little waterfall near some cliff rocks, which we named the "faery pond" for my niece. I like to think that there were little water nymphs dancing in the running water, splashing and singing with each other.

Taking my niece to the beach is always a lovely experience because she is so fascinated by the world around her, she's looking through a magnifying glass that intensifies the world! She particularly enjoyed making shapes and marks in the sand with stones, although I have no idea what she was drawing! She loved sifting through stones with us, looking for sea glass.

Unfortunately, we didn't find great big chunks of sea glass that I've seen other people find, but we did find some adorable tiny pieces, in green and clear colours. I also ended up collecting some purple-toned stones as I was particularly drawn to purple amethyst crystals at that time, so I didn't end up leaving with nothing! No crabs though sadly. Sea glass hunting is a great Summerween activity for any Sea Witch!

70s/80s Slasher Summer

Now I know I've just said that I'm excited to embrace my "Sea Witch" summer, but I've seen a new aesthetic trend floating around on TikTok that I also think will be fun to partake in! I'm a big believer in letting your interests influence your style. There're a few variations of this aesthetic which includes:

- Cryptidcore summer.
- 70s Texas Chainsaw Massacre slasher summer.
- Final Girl Summer.
- 80s Small Town summer.

All of these have similar vibes, so you could lean in heavy to any of them! The general vibe is classic *Friday the 13th* summer camp, jumping into lakes, telling ghost stories around the campfire, being stalked by a masked killer, torches that mysteriously break without reason, etc. As a spooky girl this aesthetic really resonates with me! I of course love *Stranger Things*, which is a perfect mash-up of Cryptidcore and 80s Small Town with a dash of monster hunting.

Summer/sleepaway camps are a very common thing in America, to my knowledge we don't have summer camps in the UK, although I did go to a "summer club" when I was a kid, but I returned home at the end of every day! Summer camps involve staying away in log cabins, usually near lakes with huge forests to set the background. You'd spend days taking part in team-building activities, sports, arts and crafts etc. Night-time brought telling ghost stories around a campfire, toasting marshmallows or "s'mores" as they call them, singing songs or playing hide and seek in the dark!

I say I've never had the "Summer Camp" experience; however, I went on a school trip to France when I was in Year 9 or 10. It was specifically a water sports trip which I was shocked I even agreed to go on, I don't do sports. We travelled to this picturesque sports camp in the French countryside, which did indeed have log cabins, and a lake close by! I suppose you could say I did have the "Slasher Summer" experience, in France!

A couple of memories that really cemented this was completing an orienteering activity. We had to walk a trail to find tree flags, we were in groups of 3 or 4, walking through the silent French countryside, through the woods and of course us being daft teenagers took any opportunity to spook each other, I swear I saw **The Woman in Black** in the woods! We also played "Capture the Flag" in the woods (I think I just ran in the opposite direction if anyone came near me!). We canoed, like actually **canoed** across the lake! I've just realised that I probably will never canoe again in my lifetime. What a trip...

Building your summer:

Because I love letting films and books influence my everyday life, I thought I would give you some media recommendations that will help romanticise your Slasher Summer in the best possible way!

Just imagine that you are about to go to that very popular summer camp where nothing bad ever happens! *Winks at camera*.

Wardrobe:

To capture the look of the "80s Camp Counsellor" I would recommend wearing denim shorts (the more denim the better!), baseball or striped t-shirts, vests, baseball caps, sneakers etc. Really let your imagination go wild but remember to think about the weather. Remember your suncream for those sweaty days! Sunglasses are also recommended, to look over and judge unruly campmates!

Books:

I've compiled a list of books that you could read to drive those Final Girl vibes. If you're more into horror books than films then I feel like this section will be for you! If opportunity knocks, then reading outdoors; by a firepit, in a tent etc will also capsulate those slasher camp vibes! Just be aware of your surroundings, and any strangers in hockey masks!

- Kill River
- Shock Waves
- Wonderland
- Tastes like Candy

- Cotton Candy Massacre
- Final Girl Support Group
- Camp Slaughter
- Final Girls

Film and TV

Alternatively, if you're a horror film binger I've found a list of films that you can curl up and watch on a stormy summer night, with thunder crashing and that summer rain lashing at your windows, but what's that at the window... it can't be, it's- Noooooo!........

Sorry, got a bit too into that narrative!

- AHS: 1984
- IT 1 and 2
- Stranger Things: Season 3
- Friday the 13th
- Texas Chainsaw Massacre
- Pool Party Massacre
    - X

- Jeepers Creepers
- Sleepaway Camp
- The Final Girls
- Fear Street: 1978
- Cabin in the Woods
- Cheerleader Camp

A few songs that I've found being played over these Slasher Summer edits include:

- Rock Me Amadeus
- Girls on Film
- Southern Nights
- Don't Fear the Reaper

- Burn Your House Down
- Owner of a Lonely Heart

Nothing says summer like a banging summer playlist/soundtrack! All of the best 80s films have amazing soundtracks and they always resonate after I've watched the film. For example, I'll always associate Cyndi Lauper's "Good Enough" with *The Goonies*. Speaking of *The Goonies*, it is essentially a Cryptidcore summer film, but with Italian pirates! It has kids riding on bikes, pirate shops, treasure, adventurous hijinks... I watched it so many times in my childhood!

International Pineapple Day (27th June)

The Jack-O-Pineapple is another classic Summerween fruit! When I was a kid, eating pineapple would often make me act "hyper". I don't know why! It was like getting a Gremlin wet, all hell would break loose! Nowadays, pineapple does not affect me in a hyperactive manner, I'm more mature than that!

If you enjoy the sweet tastes of pineapple, for a Summerween activity if you're feeling creative you could try and carve a pineapple in the style of a pumpkin. I've only ever done this with a watermelon (and it was extremely hard!) but I reckon you could try and do this too. Be aware that it requires a lot of scooping pineapple guts and chunks and will pump up your arm muscles!

For a simpler Summerween recipe you could make the Disney Parks "Dole Whip" ice-cream which includes:

- Pineapple juice
- Frozen/Fresh Pineapple chunks
- Vanilla ice-cream

Blend all of these ingredients together and it will make a refreshing Summerween treat, bonus points if you serve it in a spooky glass/pineapple glass! If you want to go even simpler you could literally just have pineapple chunks in a spooky bowl as a light snack, or tinned pineapple is even sweeter! The choice is yours.

The Haunted Hoppings!

"Round and round like a horse on a carousel, we go...You must be this tall to ride this ride at the carnival...this horse is too

slow, we're always this close, almost, almost, we're a Freakshow."

Melanie Martinez- Carousel.

Summerween is not just beach picnic season, but also funfair season! If you live in the Northeast of England then you are probably aware of what "The Hoppings" is. In fact, you've probably been a few times in your life. The Hoppings is a travelling funfair that has pitched up on the Town Moor (yes, ironically where the witch trials were held!) every June for **141 years!** It was just like any other funfair, with rides and rollercoasters, stalls to win prizes and lots of delicious food. Here's a few historical funfair facts for you:

- The first Hoppings took place in 1882, and featured activities like pole leaping, tug of war, skipping competitions, bike races etc.
- The name "Hoppings" refers to the kind of dancing that happened there.
- Between 1914-1918 when World War I took place, The Hoppings was actually moved to Jesmond Dene for a period of time, and when it was over it moved back to the Town Moor, its rightful home!
- In 1958, Hook-a-Duck was introduced as a stall.
- In 1951 we saw the first Rotor Spinning Wall ride.
- The first Ghost Train was designed in 1930 by Joseph Emberton and was featured at Blackpool Pleasure Beach.

The one thing I always remember about The Hoppings is the smell of hot dogs and fried onions. It's enough to make your mouth water! Walking around in the sunshine (if you're lucky!) riding on the Waltzer or the Magic Mouse, gorging on candyfloss. Sometimes it could get a little too expensive, my Mam would always offer me an alternative to going there. There's just something about the thrills and chills of the funfair.

I bet you've all been waiting for.... **The spooky part!!!!!** It wouldn't be a section of this book without some haunting history now would it? I suppose you could say this is spooky. Gosh darn it, we will make it spooky! So, according to local legend, years ago a Gypsy visiting the Hoppings was thrown out (reasons unknown) and in a fit of rage she cursed the fair to be doomed with rain and hail every year that it visits. It's a running joke that whenever the fair pitches up, it starts raining every day. It's true! The funfair was actually called off one year for the severe weather. There's also rumours of a witch frequenting the grounds, but my sources are a bit hazy on that one.

Being the spooky queen that I am, this year when I went I decided to hunt out all of the ghost trains, I am ashamed to admit that a few years ago when I last went there, I closed my eyes on the ghost train! Even the spookiest of people still get scared sometimes! Altogether I managed to count about 6 Ghost Trains. They all had the classic spray-painted horror icons adorning the ride, skeletons hung outside, the sounds of Vincent Price's laugh in *Thriller* jingling out from them. There were also two new additions that I don't remember seeing last time. The first was a Frankenstein's Monster statue stood outside the ride (each one missing a hand) and I couldn't resist getting a photo with them! There was also a ride attendee dressed in a skeleton costume, climbing on the back of the ghost cars. One of them waved at me and I fangirled a bit!

The Ghost Train is definitely the best ride to live your spooky adventure on. Because I like to theme everything with everything, I bought myself a Ghost Train pin (from *Peachy Mountain* on Etsy) that I wore to the Hoppings. Adding little accessories like this can really make you feel the full fantasy. I also brought the books that I mentioned in the *Slasher Summer* section; *The Cotton Candy Massacre, Kill River* and *Tastes Like Candy*. These are all theme park reads with a gory slasher twist that you can read to get in the mood for the funfair. They also possibly include clowns if you're into them, I know not everyone is. As you can tell I've fell deep into the *Slasher Summer* genre!

Summerween- July (Picnic Month)

Now we have a whole month dedicated to picnics! Although it is fun having picnics in Autumn and Spring, beach picnics and barbeques hit totally different! It's warm outside, the sun is shining, the sky is blue, the barbeque is smoking… what a perfect day!

A picnic fit for a Sea Witch!

I thought I would save this idea specifically for July rather than in National Picnic Day in Springoween. I like to make every activity that I do special or "extra" as some people say. For this picnic you want to resurrect something akin to Ursula herself from the hellish pit at the bottom of the sea yourself!

For your picnic outfit I would wear purple or black, a beach dress moment would fit in perfectly, with octopus or shell accessories. Having an extravagant outfit can make you feel so confident in yourself. Sea Witches are confident, so you can be too!

Your picnic menu can be simple, by going to a fish and chip shop on the coast and buying lunch there with your favourite order of choice (I change between loving a battered sausage and being obsessed with a fish cake!) or you can create your own menu. I would personally go with seafood. Salmon and cream cheese sandwiches in spooky shapes, crab sticks and seafood dip, prawns, sushi etc. Include blue mocktails for the ocean colours, salt & vinegar and prawn cocktail crisps (we also have snack crisps in the UK, that are salt & vinegar flavoured and shaped like fish and chips!). Seafood can be something people either love or hate, so if you do not like it, feel free to change the menu in any way you like.

Lastly is your overall décor and activities. I've seen online you can get a "skeleton sand mould" (might need to search hard for this!) which could be a fun activity reminiscent of making sandcastles as a child. You could also go shell hunting, fishing in rock-pools, cave exploring etc. There are so many things to do at the beach! Let the calming waves carry your worries away and wash your mind clean of stress.

Quest Achieved:
Dungeons and Dragons experience 2022

"Maybe tomorrow we can play DnD?"

Will Byers, Stranger Things.

It all started when my cousin asked us (my other cousin and her friend) if we wanted to play DnD. We are all big fans of Stranger Things so seeing them play DnD and battle monsters from that universe seemed like a great idea! Maybe not the monsters' part... My cousin had already done research into it and was starting to set up her own campaign and character profile. I vaguely understood the rules, but if I'm being perfectly honest, the game freaked me out. Not for the reasons that you might think (Vecna is one scary dude). It was the dice. Basically, in DnD, you use a seven dice set with various numbered sides e.g., there's a twenty-sided dice called the D20. You roll the dice to conjure up different outcomes during battle. This was explained to me, but it still confused me. There's also a lot of addition involved when adding up your statistics for your character. I found all of this very hard because I struggle with Dyscalculia. If you haven't heard of it it's similar to Dyslexia, but it effects your mental arithmetic and understanding of numbers. I struggled with it a lot in school, getting extra maths lessons for support and disappearing for them in between lessons.

Now being faced with a bunch of numbered dice terrified me. I didn't want to stumble or seem like I couldn't count. Thankfully my teammates were very supportive. They were patient and didn't rush me when I was struggling. That's what being part of a party is all about! Supporting each other throughout your adventures. Running through our DnD sessions was always so much fun. We would get into the craziest situations; with the most insane dialogue you could imagine.

Let's start back at the beginning! On a particularly tipsy night at my cousin's flat we decided to create our characters. We chose our class, race and background and what our names were. I decided I wanted to be a mermaid, a witchy mermaid! I ended up choosing to be a "Merfolk Druid" named Melusine. The name actually means "a female spirit of fresh water in a holy well or river", which I thought was very fitting! My party members names are Siofra, Ace and Sorrow. Within our party we have our Dungeon Master, a Paladin Elf, a Sorcerer Tiefling and me, the Merfolk Druid! We get up to all sorts of nonsense. Searching for trolls and pillaging villages just because we can!

I thought I'd share a snippet of one of our DnD sessions. I was given a 'Character Journal' and my own set of dice for my birthday from my cousins. Everyone has a journal that we use to write in notes from each session, our profile, character statistics, spells etc. I treat each session as a way to write down everything we do in story format. It gets a little hard sometimes, but I've gotten used to quickly scribbling our adventures down on paper. So, here is a scene that was particularly fun to take part in!

"We head to the Sleeping Giant; people lie in doorway wearing shiny red cloaks. They mock us. Sorrow pokes them. A fight breaks out. 4 rough'ns, 4 against 3. They attack us with slurs, disgusting behaviour! I use my spear and attack saying, "I'm going to gut you like a fish, because you called me a fish!". I hit but do no damage. Siofra almost gets punched in the face. One's nose is broken. Upper cuts and misses. I pull my spear out of him. Siofra dodges a punch. I get hit but still have my spear. He then goes for Siofra and Sorrow. Siofra bursts victim

into flames using "searing smite" spell. I shift into a wolf; I bite and writhe his groin and try to rip his privates off. Goes for Sorrow with short sword. Pierces in stomach. The fire victim saves himself. I try to jump and one's head off and miss. Siofra goes to punch in the chest. I go for the head and a swing around. I grab by leg, thump and kill. Save him for parts later. I go for Sorrow's attacker. Swing and thump work well.... Siofra squeezes him to death as he is now useless. We then take their clothes and weapons, gowns to blend in. I have a feast on the bodies and then we conceal them. We head back to the tavern, I'm in my human form again. The tavern cheers for us! Elsa gives us an ale on the house. We then have a long rest."

As you can see from this short scene, we are quite a savage bunch! It's funny because when I was creating my character and hyping myself up for the game I was thinking I would be a 'damsel in distress' type character, doing no wrong and just blending in. But honestly, once my cousin turns her DnD playlist on and the battle music plays, something inside me awakens! Apparently it's a rampant mermaid who can turn into a wolf who likes to rip victim's privates off! Melusine is wild...

World UFO Day (2nd July)

Do aliens walk among us?... It's hard to tell! A lot of people (including my Mam) hardcore believe that aliens exist. As well as UFOs. If you don't know what a UFO is, it basically stands for "Unidentified Flying Object". Like when you're walking home from work, and you look up into the sky, you see a little beaming light that looks like it could be a plane, just think, it might be a UFO... Just imagine, aliens in that vehicle, flying above our heads. They might be green with black eyes the size of dinnerplates, or they might look just like us! You never know...

You can celebrate this day in whatever way you like. You could grab some alien-themed snacks and watch *The X Files*, *Red Dwarf* or *Doctor Who* for those extraterrestrial vibes. You could go out and go UFO-spotting in the night sky, you could make your own tinfoil hat that attracts alien activity. Do whatever you like! There's plenty of stories online of people who have had alien-abducting experiences so you could spook yourself and read those with all the lights off. But remember, don't answer your front door to any black-eyed children...

Alice in Wonderland Day (4th July)

Many years ago, on the 4th of July, Lewis Carroll told the story of *Alice's Adventures in Wonderland* to a small child named Alice Liddell before deciding to write it down. Thus, becoming one of the most bizarre children's classics in history. I personally love *Alice in Wonderland* and have done since I was a child. I remember watching the Disney cartoon and being both fascinated and weirded out by the story. There are so many different adaptations of the story, I feel like it might be one of the most adapted children's books of all time! I might be wrong, but I've never seen so many versions of it. Including a version from 1915, 1931, 1933, 1949, all through the 60s, to the 80s and 90s as well as some made-for-TV movies in the early 2000s and the Tim Burton adaptations in 2010 and 2016.

I've spoken about how to celebrate *Alice in Wonderland* a few times in this book. Including how to have an Alice tea party, with spooky Red Queen vibes. The Wonderland universe is very easy to twist into something unnatural and scary. It already is! Talking cats, snooty flowers, playing croquet with flamingos... When I was in secondary school I went through a phase of being obsessed with "fairytale retellings". In the 2010s there were a few that turned classic fairytales into YA books. I had read quite a few at this point when I discovered one more, that was about *Alice in Wonderland*…

Splintered by AG Howard (2013)

Splintered is the story of Alyssa Gardner, who is the descendant of Alice Liddell. Alyssa can hear the whispers of bugs and flowers, which is what landed her mother in a mental hospital years before. But Alyssa knows that the family curse has been passed down to her from her ancestor Alice, who first fell down the rabbit hole into Wonderland herself. Alyssa didn't believe any of it until she learns that she has to descend down the dark hole herself in order to save her family and write some wrongs of the past. This is a YA supernatural/paranormal romance that clouds over your memories of Wonderland and makes them so much darker than you remembered…

The **stress** I had of trying to find and order this book was a joke. My school librarian was a absolute saint and managed to order a hardback version for me to read. I still love her so much for that. I read the book and absolutely loved it. It was dark and twisted and very creepy, with strong themes of bugs and flowers. Who knew that years later in 2022 I would develop a hyper fixation for mushrooms! All of the characters were not what I remembered even the March Hare was now a zombified rabbit monstrosity!

Even at the age of 26, I still have a special place in my heart for fairytale retellings. There are even more creepy retellings specifically of *Alice in Wonderland* including *Alice in Zombieland, After Alice, Heartless, Alice in Borderland* etc. If you've already had your tea party, you could definitely have a cosy afternoon reading one of these retellings or watching the Tim Burton version as it definitely has scary vibes.

Ghoulish Gift Guide:

- Tropikilla Pin collection (from *Rotten Flamingos*). I actually own a few prints already from this Etsy shop. It combines pink and spooky together which makes the products stand out! This pin collection includes a pink skull palm tree, a spooky pina colada, a pink drink out of a skull (with matching umbrellas), and a skeleton flamingo! I love the girly side of spook! I also got a free "Hot Ghoul Summer" print!
- Ghost Train pin (from *Peachy Mountain*) I bought this specifically to wear to the Hoppings. I love the creepy carnival vibes!
- Frankencat Jack O'Melon pin (from *Dolly Cool*). I love the motif of the "Jack O'Melon" and to see it with a cat?! Even cuter. This is also a wooden pin; I don't own many wooden pins but it's nice to have variety of materials.
- Summerween TBR bookmark (from *Bookmarks by Alicia*). This is made for the Summerween readathon that I take part in every year. It's nice to have a memento that I can keep and use in each readathon!
- Summerween Bookmarks (from *SandStarArt*). I have so many bookmarks from this shop, I just love the illustration style! The two I have depicted a ghost reading a True Crime novel on top of a sandcastle and the second is a triple spooky ice-scream!

Land Ahoy Haunting History:

"I've got a jar of dirt!"

Captain Jack Sparrow, Pirates of the Caribbean.

Pirates. Yes, pirates. Of all the things that we have discussed in this book, did you think pirates would make the cut? Pirates are weirdly an excellent Summerween character! They sail the Seven Seas, pillaging and murdering, stealing and scavenging.

Skull and crossbones adorn their ships; they probably drink out of the skulls of their victims to be fair. Pirates are seriously **spooky**. And what else comes with pirates? Pirate ghosts and ghost ships. Very much reminds me of *The Goonies*. I grew up with the *Putrid Pirates* segment on *Horrible Histories* so that was my blueprint for pirates!

Now because I love including local history, I have found that the Northeast is home to some dastardly pirate stories! Not all of these stories are concrete, some still have a lot of mystery swirling around them, but I still thought the legends seemed very interesting! Move aside Captain Jack, we have our own motley skeleton crew!

Spottee the Bandit

Spottee was a pirate who lived in the cave's entrance of Roker Park in Sunderland. He wore a spotted shirt, giving him the nickname "Spottee the Bandit". He was a typical pirate, full of mischief. He liked lighting fires in his cave, which would trick passing sailors, who thought they were heading into the harbour. While they were distracted he would loot their ship for treasure. If you happen to be on the Sunderland coast on a stormy night, you might be able to spot his ghost, still causing mischief!

Edward Robinson

On the banks of the River Tyne lived our very own Geordie pirate named Edward Robinson. After his first act of crime involved slitting a man's throat and dumping his body in the river, Edward ran away and became a pirate, joining the famous Blackbeard's crew. He was involved in many swashbuckling adventures, searching for treasure, murdering people where it was convenient. After getting into an argument with the captain he was marooned on a desert island, fighting for his very life before being rescued. Lesson learned: **never** piss off Blackbeard!

Pirate Grave

The oldest church in Northumberland is named St Mary's Churchyard. It was built in the 11th Century and decommissioned in 1974. To this day, the churchyard is still intact, if a little weather-beaten. Look closer and you will find the infamous 'pirate grave', as it is known locally, as it features the  image of "skull and crossbones". Nobody knows exactly how old the grave is, but the agreement is it definitely belongs to a pirate. The skull and crossbones were actually translated to "memento mori" in Latin which means "remember you will die". Very popular to decorate gravestones within the 17th-18th century. So, whether or not this actually belonged to a real-life pirate is a mystery...

Grave clean-ups

Not necessarily pirate themed, but I found this article on the internet and I found it extremely interesting. A team of volunteers have recently began uncovering hundreds of unrecorded graves in St Mary's Old Town Churchyard in the Isles of Scilly.

A couple named Lindsay and Brian Sandford started the project during the 2021 lockdown, and have continued it, bringing the whole community together. Ms Sandford has actually written three books, recording the unknown lives of the people buried in the churchyard. 850 headstones and plaques have been counted, some including mass graves. 335 people actually died when the SS Schiller sank off Scilly in 1835.

Just hearing about this historical project is fascinating. To see a community come together to uncover all of these people's lost stories is such a beautiful tribute. One grave story I thought would tie into here was: Captain Peter Lambton. He was of course a ship's captain, buried at the Old Town on the 20[th of] January 1781. Apparently he was captured, ransomed and killed by French pirates.

The Jingling Geordie

This person is another character with a mysterious identity. Some say he was a fettered (chained around the ankles) pirate/smuggler who lured ships onto the rocks and used his cave (known as the "Jingling Geordie Hole") to store his treasure. This cave is located in between King Edward's Bay and Tynemouth Castle. The 'jingling' part of his name refers to the clanking noise that the chains around his ankles made as he moved around. Some say you can still him hear him rattling around his cave, sorting out his supposed treasure…

Cullercoats Faery Caves

As I've said previously, I spent a lot of my childhood at Cullercoats Beach in the summer, looking for seashells and teetering on the edges of the caves. Now as I look into this, the folklore and history of the caves becomes more fantastical than I ever could have imagined! Tales of pirate ghosts, Jenny Greenteeth, smugglers, demons, dragons and wizards have floated around for years! Unfortunately, there isn't a lot of specific information that I can find about these caves. I feel like this could be more of a "leave it up to you" situation. Whatever you believe, believe it! One thing that we do know for certain, is that a ship named the "Fairy Maid" was wrecked in the harbour in July 1899 (ooh July, spooky!). Was this ship run by ghost pirates, smugglers, water faeries? It's up to you, matey…

Halloween Hunting begins…

Here is a brief timeline of how Halloween Hunting normally begins in the UK! There's definitely a system that happens when it comes to shops releasing their Halloween stock. Here's what I spotted in 2023 when I was on the Halloween hunt…

- 17th June: Nothing yet.
- 21st June: mini–Code Autumn in Primark
- 6th July: Code Orange in TKMaxx and HomeSense (Metrocentre)
- 29th July: more stock found in Primark.
- 12th August: Primark homeware
- 12th August: Asda homeware
- 15th August: B&M and Home Bargains
- 18th August: Tesco!

Summerween: August (My Birthday month!)

"Did my invitations disappear, why'd I put my heart on every cursive letter? It's my party and I'll cry if I want to, cry if I want to (cry cry cry), I'll cry until the candles burn down this place, I'll cry until my pity parties in flames!" Melanie Martinez- Pity Party.

Dear Birthdayween,

Happy Birthday to me, Happy Birthday to me, Happy Birthday to Megan, Happy Birthday to me! Yes, I am a Leo... I couldn't not include a section dedicated to my birthday! Birthdays are so special; I know some people don't like to make a fuss about their birthdays, but I personally do! Having a love of spooky things is also helpful when it's your birthday because you can make it as fun and scary as you like!

Pumpkin balloons, creepy cake, scary streamers are all symbols of Birthdayween! Birthdayween definitely is not recognised as an actual part of the 'weens' but I think it's an extra exciting activity to have. What's the point in not making life as exciting as possible?! Gone are the days of birthday parties in McDonald's, or the infamous Burger King parties (the early 2000s were crazy okay). All I want from now until I hopefully reach 100 is spooky parties. For my 25th birthday my family very kindly put on a "Halloween tea" at my sister's house. She stuck little bats to the doors, pumpkins dotted around, my niece's feet were turned into ghost bunting, and we had "Boo" balloons on the table! I also had a ghost cake and cupcakes with horror icons sticking out of them! *Hocus Pocus* was also played in the background on the telly.

It was like a little slice of heaven! That was my first spooky birthday that wasn't organised by me, and I highly enjoyed it. The year after I even had a mushroom-themed family tea because of my obsession with the fungi. In this section I want to talk about ways that you can celebrate your birthday in the creepiest way possible. I'll be including my two favourite films e.g., *Hocus Pocus* and *Shaun of the Dead* and how you can turn them into killer birthday themes! Hopefully one day I'll be able to turn them into reality and have a *Shaun* or *Hocus Pocus* party, and you're all invited!!!

National Colouring Day (2ⁿᵈ August)

A few years ago, there was the trend of "adult colouring books" that swept over everyone. I hadn't coloured anything in since I was in primary school. I used to not like colouring in if I'm honest! I could never stay in the lines, but when you're colouring in your own book, there's no one to tell you that you aren't doing it right! To celebrate the art of not caring about what people think, and indulging in feeling like a kid again, here is my collection of spooky colouring books!

1. Hocus Pocus. This was an obvious purchase. I had seen it circling online for a few weeks, last seen in The Works but I had yet to find it. And then one joyous day I was in the shop, and I spotted it! I love seeing illustrations of the Hocus Pocus characters, and the style of this book is really refreshing! Loads of fun pages to colour in.
2. The Nightmare Before Christmas. Another spooky Disney classic. Great present for someone for Creepmas! Variety of images and illustrations.
3. Let's Summon Demons. I love Stephen Rhodes' illustrative style. He pokes fun at wholesome message-

driven vintage children's books and replaces them with quotes such as "Eat Your Greens" with Big Foot in the background, or "Let's Have a Séance" activities for children. There are also other activities in this book like crosswords and word searches.

4. Where's the Zombie? Not actually a colouring book but a gnarly activity book, a grisly take on "Where's Wally" but spotting festering zombies instead.
5. Spooky Halloween. This is a generic Halloween book but with some cute spooky illustrations in it. Nice for any fan of the season.

National Watermelon Day (3rd August)

"I carried a watermelon."

Baby Houseman, Dirty Dancing.

The Jack O'Melon is a very popular motif for Summerween. It's a juicy fruit that others and I enjoy eating on a hot day. It's also conveniently shaped similar to a pumpkin. When I heard that people actually try to carve them, I knew it was my turn to try. I tried this for the Summerween readathon in 2021. It was actually quite a fun activity to do, I recommend trying it!

Firstly, grab yourself a juicy watermelon. I tried to go for a particularly round guy but whatever shape you like. Secondly, follow the same method that you use in pumpkin carving, e.g., cut the top off and start scooping, imagine you are Leatherface... I used a spoon to scoop the innards out but anything that will be comfortable in your hand.

Be warned, Jack O'Melon scooping requires **a lot** of muscle work! You might need to take a few breaks in between, I was knackered! I scooped all of my innards into a separate bowl so that I could use them for later. Once your melon is totally empty you can get to carving your pumpkin face! I went for the classic triangular eyes and mouth, but you can choose anything you like. When you're done, pop the lid back on and marvel in your creation!

Jack O'Melon slushie

Using the innards, I decided to make myself a watermelon slushie! I just blended the watermelon with some ice, added a few strawberries and fizzy sweets on top and I ended up with a delicious drink to have when finishing my book for Summerween! You could alternatively turn this into a smoothie, add some other fruits that complement the watermelon. This was the perfect cold drink to have on a Summerween day, and I highly recommend making one yourself!

The Addams Family musical (14th August 2022)

"It's family first, family last and family by and bye. When you're an Addams, the standard answers don't apply. When you're an Addams, you do what Addams do or die!"

"When You're an Addams" the *Addams Family Musical*.

I first heard about this musical from watching Carrie Hope Fletcher play Wednesday Addams in the UK tour and she vlogged behind the scenes for her YouTube channel. I unfortunately couldn't get tickets to see her but magically in 2022, my friend Hannah and I went to the Tyne Theatre to see an amateur production of it! Being the huge fan of the Addams Family that I was, I was so excited to see it.

If you haven't already seen it, it depicts an 18-year-old Wednesday, who falls in love with a 'normal' boy and the chaos that ensues as the boy's family meets the kooky Addams family. Wednesday has always been my favourite member of the family, but this musical made me fall in love with Fester and Gomez even more. I also liked the introduction of the Beineke family. Particularly Lucas, brought another side to

Wednesday that we never really see. A soft and fluffy side! All of this is brought on because she falls hard for Lucas. We also get to see the "Addams ancestors", long-dead relatives come back to life.

A slight criticism that I always find when we see Wednesday as a teenager is the relationship with her mother, Morticia is always pretty toxic. I suppose it's quite realistic in that sense, because a lot of relationships with teens and their mams are quite strained as they get older. But once I would love to see Morticia and Wednesday have a more positive relationship, when they don't argue all the time!

The musical also has a ton of original songs like Pulled, Crazier than You, When You're an Addams, One Normal Night, Just Around the Corner, Full Disclosure etc. I had already been listening to the soundtrack because of Carrie, so I was really excited to hearing the songs live, and they did not disappoint! Pulled was probably my favourite ballad, but Crazier Than You was such a fun song, and Just Around the Corner became a new favourite!

My Birthday! (17th August)
You've Got Cake on You

This party theme is of course inspired by my favourite zombie film *Shaun of the Dead*. This idea can be very simple with drops of Shaun throughout. Start with a zombie base e.g. zombie tableware, backdrop (to make it look like zombies are trying to burst through your doors), zombie balloons, caution tape, blood bags etc. Most Halloween shops have ranges such as severed body parts (fake of course) that you could scatter around the room. Even play your own real-life *Operation* by hiding different body parts around the room, see how long it takes for you to find all of the parts to make up your zombified victim! Dress code: zombies or zombie slayers!

Then add more touches of Shaun. Make a "bar" area that looks like it was pulled straight out of the Winchester Pub with beer on tap and an array of pub snacks like pork cracklings or peanuts (check for allergies). Hang up a dart board, if you have room you could add in a snooker table as well. Add a "weapons box" maybe near the front door of random objects such as odd shoes, a pillow, a spatula, a book, shampoo bottle etc and see which weapons your guests will choose during the zombie apocalypse. Have *Shaun of the Dead* playing on your telly in the background, I feel like it adds extra ambience to have the inspiration on!

Who Lit the Black Flamed Birthday Candle?

This is inspired of course by *Hocus Pocus*, possibly my favourite film of all time. I've mentioned earlier about creating a *Hocus Pocus* picnic, and I suppose this is pretty similar. Start with a basic witch theme, lots of purple and black, cauldrons and spiders hanging from the ceiling in the form of paper streamers, lots of lit candles (if you have any autumnal candles this will be perfect for creating that Halloween atmosphere! Have a rack of broomsticks (most Pound shops/supermarkets bring them out around Halloween) near your front door so your guests can grab their mode of transportation home.

Ask your guests to come dressed in their best witchy attire or any character from the film, you could of course have your pick of any of the Sanderson Sisters. My personal favourite is Sarah Sanderson, I relate to her being the youngest sister (and the ditsiest) plus I live for her long wavy hair and her **dress!!!** Have trick-or-treat buckets filled with Halloween sweeties dotted around so that you can get your fill of that sweet candy!

National Black Cat Appreciation Day (17th August)

I love black cats. My cousin had a chunky black cat called Salem. I remember him so well. He was so chilled and calm.

One day we were pet-sitting for them at their house and he came and sat on my lap for the first time. I was so happy! Unfortunately, not everyone loves black cats, and a lot of people think they're 'bad luck'. That's why we celebrate Black Cat Appreciation Day, to show that these gorgeous cats are just as special as any other cat.

A while ago I was working on another creative project, and I created a fictional cat café, named "Binx and Boops". As you can guess, this café was witchy themed, housing mostly black cats with spooky names. To show our appreciation, I thought I'd include an extract of the description of the café that I wrote! I wish it was real...

Binx and Boops...

The cat café was located on a strange back alley in our local shopping centre. It was like a real life Diagon Alley! There were vintage clothing shops 'nerdy' gaming/gift shops, a fortune teller, a board game café, herbal tearooms etc., However, we weren't stopping at those.

Our destination was a quaint little café on the corner with a purple awning, a black front door and a big bay window. There was also a blackboard sign outside with "Binx and Boops" written on it in italics. As we entered into the little porch we were told to take off our shoes at the door, just like any other cat café, and then we entered...

There were cats everywhere! Obviously, but I was starstruck! A lot of the furry creatures were chilling on a big cat tree in the middle of the room, that looked like a old, gnarled tree with soft cat bed cauldrons hanging from the branches. The cats were also sleeping in pumpkin or haunted house cat dens or lounging on patterned bean bags dotted around. The walls were rusted brick with two walls filled with framed pictures. There was a big vintage bookcase filled with books, a blood red fluffy rug, jars of candles and bat-shaped fairy lights...The 9 black cats were named Wednesday, Salem, Emily Bronte, Oreo, Poe, Victor, Sooty, Eleven and Captain Hook.

Burger Day (24th August)

Time for a Halloween barbeque! You can't do Summerween and not have a bad-ass barbeque. I'm taking this inspiration from a TikTok I saw last year. Here are a few ways you can spookify your barbeque!

- Monster burgers: use two olives on cocktail sticks and stick them in the top of your bun. Have a gherkin stick out of the burger as a tongue, tomato salsa for blood. If you're creative you could try and dye the bun black also.
- Mummy sausage rolls. Wrap pastry in mummy-style wrap around a sausage. Dip into a delicious dip or sauce of your choice.
- Bloody finger hot dogs. Carve finger wrinkles into hot dog sausages and place in your bun, add tomato sauce for extra bloodiness.
- Pumpkin cheeseburgers. Another alternative to a burger is to carve a Jack O'Lantern face into a slice of cheese to place on your burger.
- Dead Man's ribs. Place on a wooden slab in the shape of a pair of ribs, add a knife sticking out, tomato in the middle for the heart and salsa for you've guessed it, blood!

International Bat Night (27th August)

The Bat Night has taken place on the last weekend of August (24th-25th) since 1997 (ironically the year I was born!). Its aim is to spread awareness of bats and their kind. Groups of park rangers, community groups and bat groups come together to watch bats over our natural environment. They also work with the "Bat Conservation Trust" to further spread this awareness.

Creepy Corn Maze (28th August)

At the end of August in 2022, myself, my sister, niece, and Mam decided to go sunflower picking at Brockbushes Farm & Teashop. We had previously been here for strawberry and pumpkin picking, so sunflower picking was a first-time activity! I couldn't imagine what they would look like, but it was such a mesmerising scene! Miles of bright yellow sunflowers, taller than me stretched across the farm. It was gorgeous just to walk through the flower fields, with cute little props dotted in and out, e.g. a toadstool, a little old-fashioned playhouse, a tin man etc. But here's where it gets spooky...

I love taking book-themed photos wherever I go, especially if I visit a spooky place. I couldn't actually find a book that had the word "sunflower" in it. I was going to go for a rom-com or women's fiction, but I had nothing in my library that went with it! So, I chose "Clown in a Cornfield" because it involved a "field" of some sort. As we were walking through the fields we stumbled upon a cornfield/maze! If you've read *Pumpkinheads* by Rainbow Rowell (an unbelievably adorable Halloween graphic novel) you'll know that corn mazes are a *big thing* in America.

I had never actually been in a corn maze before, so I was so surprised, and even more surprised that the book that I brought was set in a cornfield! You can imagine I took a lot of pictures of that book... It was so strange seeing these corn husks towering over us, looking like they were ready to be picked and ate! There were even some haybales further on in the farm, where there was a mini fairground, and we got some adorable photos of my niece silhouetted by the sun. It goes to show that you never know what is around the corner, especially in a corn maze, it could be a creepy clown...

Autumnween

August to November

Dear Autumnween,

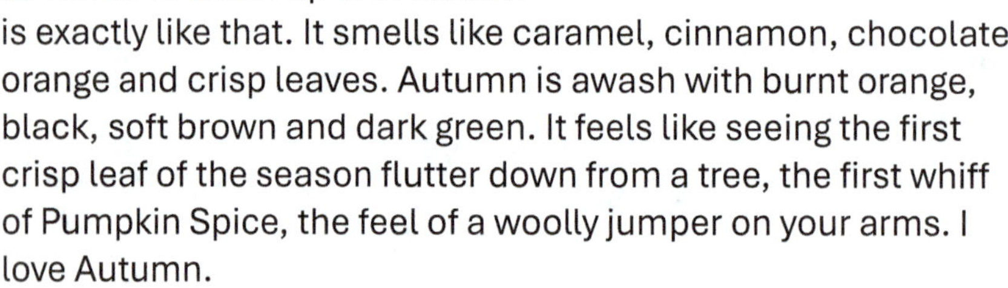

You're finally here! My dear friend from long ago… Knocking on my door on a dark and stormy evening, with a basket full of toffee apples and pumpkins. It feels like it's been too long since you were last here, we have so much to catch up on! Autumn is exactly like that. It smells like caramel, cinnamon, chocolate orange and crisp leaves. Autumn is awash with burnt orange, black, soft brown and dark green. It feels like seeing the first crisp leaf of the season flutter down from a tree, the first whiff of Pumpkin Spice, the feel of a woolly jumper on your arms. I love Autumn.

Now, you might be wondering why I'm not referring to this section as "Halloween" instead of "Autumnween". Before Halloween was here, Autumn was always here, blessing our eyes with its rustic colours. Not only do I love Halloween, but I also love Autumn. Halloween is the naughty faery, pulling tricks and hiding pumpkins for children to find. Autumn is a wispy faery, painting the leaves orange and brown and blowing cold breezes that ruffles our hair. I can't choose between the two however, I love both of them deeply!

Halloween was always such a fun experience as a child. In the late 90s/early 2000s, our go-to Halloween costume was the "bin bag witch" which consisted of a witch hat and appropriate face paint, a black bin bag with neck and arm holes cut out, plastic witch nails, that were luminous and glowed in the dark (they were like gloves for your individual fingers!) and tights. I can still distinctly remember one Halloween, standing in the kitchen with my Mam as she cut out and measured my bin liner dress. However, I also remember dressing as a "French, singing, dancing pirate". I don't know why I decided to make the pirate French, but I applaud little Megan for her creativity!

For a friend's birthday party one year in primary school (her birthday was near October) she had a party at her house. The theme was Halloween fancy dress and I have never been so jealous of a person's house than I was of her house. She lived in a stony, almost Victorian house in the middle of the woods. It was dark, mysterious and seriously spooky! We were all dressed in creepy costumes, I was wearing my sister's hand-me-down 'Lady Dracula' costume, and I'm sure at one point we actually went on a ghost walk in the woods outside her house. I really wish I had more memories and photos from this birthday party, because my Halloween-loving heart **now** would be so into a party like that!

I have to admit, I didn't really take much notice of Autumn when I was a child. To me, it was the season when it rained a lot, it was windy, and we had to bring in tins (soup, sweetcorn etc) for the school's Harvest Festival. In my simple little mind, Autumn was a weather, not a season. But now that I am in tune with my seasons, I see Autumn for all the beauty that it bestows every year. In 2022, I became, what I like to call, an **"Autumn Explorer"** which consisted of me taking photos of different elements in nature e.g., berries, mushrooms, acorns, conkers etc. I particularly enjoyed looking for mushrooms. Mushrooms make me very happy.

Autumn was also the season that "Apple-bobbing Annie" was born. I decided that my presence on the Internet would only be spooky from that day onwards! The name is a combination of my middle name 'Annie' and the Halloween activity 'apple bobbing'. When I was brainstorming a name for myself I was obviously looking at my first name Megan as an option. Unfortunately, nothing seemed to fit. I tried 'Monstruous Meg', 'Monster Meg', 'Meg in a Mask', 'PhantasMegOria', 'Meg in the Mourning' etc but none of them worked. I then moved onto my middle name. Annie was my grandma's name, weirdly enough she hated it and always asked people to call her 'Nancy' instead. But now, I wanted that name! So, I decided on Apple-bobbing Annie. It felt cute, catchy, autumnal and it had that Halloween whimsy that I love so much. I'm so happy I chose it!

This whole book has been taking us through the year, celebrating spooky in the best ways that we can, through different seasons. But ultimately, Halloween and Autumn are every creep's end goal! We itch to see the first pieces of Halloween décor hit the shelves, we thrive in cold and gloomy weather, we blast spooky music in our ears just to feel like it's Halloween. I honestly feel like Halloween isn't just a holiday, but a **feeling**. I just wish we could freeze time whenever Autumn hits. It feels like the whole world stands still. We're just living in this little bubble, surrounded by crispy leaves and lit-up pumpkins. It truly is magical!

I really hope you enjoy this section. I feel like if you cut me open, my heart would be pumpkin orange (Sorry, gruesome image!). My love of Halloween bleeds through every page in this book, and now that it's finally here. I can't contain my excitement! In this section I'll be telling of some of my favourite Halloween experiences and activities, ways that you can spread the spook, enjoy the season to the fullest of your capacity. Live it, breathe it, smell it! It's our time, ghouls! Let the undead **RISE TONIGHT!!!**

Autumnween: September (National Mushroom Month)

Back to School: Dark Academia aesthetic

I feel like the best aesthetic to fit in with Autumn is 'Dark Academia'. The best way to describe what Dark Academia means is the "romanticisation of education, literature and higher arts". It focuses on museums, galleries, Gothic literature and studying in whatever way you can. We also have the fashion aesthetic that goes with it. If you want to dress like a Dark Academia student, you could wear crisp shirts, plaid knitwear, tweed skirts/trousers, schoolgirl blazers, lace-up shoes etc.

The reason why I think this would be something that you can romanticise in September is because a lot of people are heading back to school, college, university etc. After a long summer off some people can feel stressed about heading back. Some people don't, and the idea of a new term can feel exciting. I remember feeling relatively excited about going back to school or college when I was younger. Near the end of summer, I would buy new school stationary and a new bag in preparation for the new term. I was excited to catch up with my friends, gossip about what we had done that summer and begin our new classes.

I actually miss school in general. There were rubbish parts of school but honestly, the positives outweigh the negatives. I loved starting my GCSEs in Year 8. I ended up taking Spanish, Design and Technology, Drama and Extended Project. Studying Drama was such a blessing. I was very shy around people but comfortable with my friends. Drama made me gain so much confidence. It was a whole new world! And yes, I did at one point do a play about ghosts. Would you expect anything else? Insert the script here!

After my GCSEs and the end of Year 11, I ended up staying on in school for another two years for Sixth Form e.g., Year 12 and 13. For my Sixth Form subjects I chose English Literature, English Language, Ceramics. Sixth Form is **so much harder** than GCSEs. It was a very intense part of my education, but I still ended up loving it. To further push the Dark Academia aesthetic, the first part of my English Literature course was "Gothic Literature" which meant we got to study *Frankenstein* and the works of Edgar Allan Poe. I was living my best spooky life! I also loved studying *The Tempest* by William Shakespeare, my third Shakespeare play studied in school!

Sixth Form ended and when all of my friends were heading off to university to land themselves in hundreds of pounds of debt, I decided to go to college. I went to Newcastle College and took a Level 3 Childcare course for 2 years. I was aiming for my Level 3 qualification so that I could work in a nursery or a school. Out of school, Sixth Form and college, college has to be my favourite experience! It was only 2 years, but I have such happy and daft memories from it. I remember we would go to the Chinese supermarket around the corner from the college for lunch because they did takeaway food. What I would do for a box of those chips, sweet and sour sauce, chicken balls and noodles again... sorry, got distracted there! If we were feeling cheeky and had free periods we would go to the Discovery Museum and have fun there.

I made an amazing group of friends in college; we went on some great trips (Forbidden Corner will always be my favourite place in Yorkshire). Even the course in general was great! I loved studying, our course was really interesting as I never realised just **how much** went into Childcare! One of my favourite assignments was we got to create our own thematic project. We had to plan different activities that fit into the EYFS e.g., Physical Development, Literacy, Numeracy, Expressive Arts and Design, Understanding the World etc. We could pick our own theme for the project. I'm shocked I didn't do a Halloween theme, but I did go over the top with my project! My project even won me a runner-up prize at a competition in college! Good memories...

So that's a run down of my education! I do miss studying and working towards something. I definitely have studied for this book though! If you want to romanticise Dark Academia I recommend studying. Picking a subject that is interesting to you, or a subject that you know nothing about and really digging into it. Even learning a new language! Here's some other little ways you can romanticise the aesthetic.

- Dress in plaid, dark colours, tweed and knitwear.

- Be studious, pick a subject and immerse yourself in it.
- Listen to classical music.
- Read Gothic or classic literature.
- Visit museums, libraries and galleries.

How to be an Autumn Explorer!

As I said in my love letter, in 2022 I became what I like to call an "Autumn Explorer"! I discovered so many beautiful parts of autumn that I had never paid attention to before. Now, these aren't extensive tips to be an autumn explorer, they're just little things that I spotted out and about. I loved taking photos of these to put on my Instagram, even though I am definitely not a professional photographer! So, here's some little gems of Autumn that you can keep your eye out for!

- **Berries.** Obviously different fruits grow at different times of the year e.g., strawberries in the summer, apples in the autumn etc. There are a few little trees and bushes around where I live, most of them growing out of people's garden or at the side of the road. As I went about my daily commutes e.g., to work or going about my day in general I saw the most gorgeous berries and of course I had to stop and take photos! A few kinds of berries that I saw the most were "Rosehip" and "Viburnum" in shades of rich red and purple. It just made my day seeing these little berries blessing my view!
- **Acorns/pinecones.** Am I the only person who thinks that pinecones look like hedgehogs? It reminds me of a childhood of using natural materials in arts and crafts. A pinecone's function is actually to keep a pine tree seeds safe. They close their scales in cold temperatures to protect the seeds, and then open up and release them in the warmer months as it's easy for the seed to germinate then. I just think they're such quirky little things, unlike anything I've seen before. Near my work there's a little cul-de-sac of bungalows, overlooking these bungalows there

are a tall pine trees, that constantly have fallen pinecones on the ground. I like to look for pinecones to take home with me, like spiky treasures! I used to think that they only fell during Autumn, but these pinecones cover the grass in the cul-de-sac.

- **Apples.** I feel like a lot of the time you have to drive or hunt for an apple orchard in this country. In America I know apple orchards are just as popular as pumpkin patches in Autumn. Amazingly, in my work we have a little apple tree in both of our smaller garden and three big apple trees on the school grounds. The kids always become so excited when we see the apples on the grass, I love telling them how they grow and eventually fall off the tree. It's tradition in childcare to do an abundance of apple-related crafts in Autumn. I also developed my name "Apple-bobbing Annie" from seeing the apples trees. From this and ordering a little print from a small shop. It was a black and white illustration of a line of monsters waiting to bob apples.

- **Leaves.** Now this is an obvious one. That's why Americans call Autumn "Fall" because the leaves literally fall off the trees! One of my favourite things is seeing the leaves perform. Their first act is changing colours. From luscious green to burnt orange, rusty brown and red. Their second act is falling off the trees. Turning crispy as they slowly die. The last act is known to me as "The Dance of the Leaves" as they dance and twirl in the brisk autumn wind, spinning and spiralling into tornadoes. Left behind are tall trees with skinny skeleton branches, waiting for the leaves to grow back. I like collecting leaves, pressing them between book pages or laminating them into bookmarks.

- **Mushrooms.** I don't know if it's because I wasn't paying attention in the first place, but the more mushrooms I found, the more appeared. I first spotted them around the bus terminus that I catch to work. Little button mushrooms dotted across the grass. Now don't worry, I know that many species of mushroom are toxic, so I didn't touch or ingest any, only took photos! After that I found some more larger mushrooms in the same place. I am stating here that I am not a professional or skilled mushroom forager. I'm still fairly new to learning about mushroom species so if you want to try and forage for mushrooms I would research beforehand and follow safety guidelines. It just shows that you don't need to head into the depths of the woods to find mushrooms and they can be anywhere! As I'm writing this I've found mushrooms in every season and am the proud owner of an extensive mushroom collection e.g., jewellery, ornaments, candle, prints, pins etc.

- **Pumpkins and Corn** *" *It's corn! A big gourd with knobs, it has the juice!*" *. Yes I included a TikTok sound, don't judge me! I love pumpkins. I love looking at them, I love carving them, I love holding them. I just bloody love them! They are a staple for Halloween and all of the other weens. I always thought that pumpkin patches only existed in America, until I discovered that the UK have them too! I went pumpkin picking for the first time around two years ago. It truly is a magical experience. Just ignore the cold, the mud and the grey skies. Whenever I go pumpkin picking I always imagine I'm walking around to the *Halloweentown* theme song. Corn is a different story. I've again never been in a cornfield, mostly hyped in America where they have hayrides, Halloween-themed festivities in cornfields etc. Towards the end of August last year, I went sunflower picking with my family. We were walking around the sunflower trail when we ended up in a cornfield! I was amazed, especially since I brought a copy of the book "Clown in a Cornfield" with me (I didn't have any about sunflowers!). Now I can say I've been in a pumpkin patch, and a cornfield!

International Literacy Day (8ᵗʰ September)

One of the many personal layers that goes into this book is that I am a complete bookworm. I have been ever since I was tiny. I remember the first time I was able to read a book out loud, I sat on my Granda's knee and read "Horrid Henry's Stink bomb" all the way through, without stopping! I was so proud of myself. Every school library that I visited was like a whole new world. I devoured *Lettice Rabbit* and *We're Going on a Bear Hunt* in nursery, I giggled my way through Horrid Henry in first school, I stepped into "big girl reading" in primary school when my friend introduced me to Jacqueline Wilson. I could write a whole other book about my reading journey (if I can find the notes on it!). I've definitely enjoyed spooky reading the most.

International Literacy Day isn't just about reading though, it's about making sure that everyone has basic literacy skills, and gets rid of illiteracy, dating all the way back to 1965. That's actually what I based my thematic project on in college! I named it "Encouraging Literacy Development (Education in the Community)", although I tried to cover all areas of the EYFS, fairytales and stories were the root theme. There are so many ways that you can celebrate and encourage literacy, and of course, I have to recommend some spooky ideas!

- Donate books to local classrooms. You can do this with just normal books or specifically spooky books. This will really help during Halloween season if they're looking for topic books for the autumn term. A few I can recommend are *The Graveyard Book, Coraline, The Halloween Tree, The Halloween Moon, The Haunting of Aveline Jones* etc.
- Gift a book. Wrap it up in spooky wrapping paper or fabric, with a black ribbon, maybe a little fake spider? If it's for a small child you can also do this with a picture book. I for one would be ecstatic to receive one of these! It would also make a cute Halloween present for your child or sibling.

- Start a community lending library. I've seen lots of "free little libraries" dotted about in small communities. Usually on the end of someone's drive, next to a post-box (I've even seen one *in* a telephone box, and a bus stop!) or within the local area. My cousin lives in a small village near Morpeth and round the corner from her, leading into their cul-de-sac, they have a little free library, a wooden box with a door, built like a mini treehouse. Just think, you could be the first person to start a free spooky library! I feel like you would see something like that in Stars Hollow (*Gilmore Girls*). A community who only appreciate autumnal pleasures in life, imagine going on a walk to your local coffee shop (Luke's?) to get a pumpkin spice latte, breezing past the little library, selecting a cozy novel and sitting in the local park, reading. Ah... bliss!

In 2023 I've tried to plan my year of reading out. I like to think that I'm organised and motivated, but in reality, I'm very flaky. I love the idea of planning my reading out, but when it comes to it, I feel restricted and end up just mood reading, which is also valid. Mood reading can be fun! As I'm writing this it is coming up to September, and I've only achieved one month of reading goals (May, reading *Stranger Things* themed books for a month).

As a promise to myself that I will read spookily towards the end of the year, I thought I'd write in here my Autumn reading plans! I tried to plan each month with a theme. Starting with "Cosy September" I plan on reading specifically cosy, autumnal books. I've chosen:

- After Dark with Roxie Clark
- Pumpkinheads
- Cider Mill Coven
- The Café between Pumpkin and Pie
- The Haunting of Aveline Jones.

To me these books evoke small town coziness, chilly weather, ghost stories, solving mysteries and sweet treats. If this isn't your vibe of course you can adapt and change but I just always want to feel like I'm in a *Nancy Drew* novel or an episode of *Scooby Doo*!

For October I try to go all the way! A few years ago, I picked books that were similar to my favourite childhood Halloween films, another year I read witchy books, this year I want to read books about vampires and werewolves. If you can't read about supernatural creatures in October when can you?! The answer is all year round of course.

- Mina and the Undead/Slayers (first book & sequel)
- When Life Gives You Vampires
- In Nightfall
- Squad
- Fangs
- Such Sharp Teeth
- My Roommate is a Vampire

I've mixed it up here with a couple of YA books, adult and graphic novels because it's nice to switch up your reading preferences every now and then! I don't normally read vampire or werewolf books either so I thought it would be nice to try it! I unfortunately never got into the *Twilight* series when I was a teenager (sorry, Lynsey and Louise!) so this could be the start of my vampire renaissance!

November is still in the Autumn season, and it gives me darker vibes as we're winding down the year and heading towards Yule. Because of this I've decided to read ghost books. Ghostly reads, ghost stories, 'whoooo', you get the picture! Also, side note: at the moment (August 2023) there is a trend going around where people buy thrifted (charity or vintage shop) paintings and paint ghosts and add other spooky imagery onto them! I will be doing this when I find the right painting!

- Funeral Girl
- The Dead Romantics
- Holly Horror
- The Ghost Goes to the Dogs
- The Ghosts of Howlfair

Again, another mixture of middle grade, YA, cozy mystery and adult romance. Happy Reading!

Curry & *Practical Magic* Night (15th September)

Autumn really is all about dark nights curled up in front of the telly, with blankets and hot drinks to comfort the change in weather. If you enjoy Saturday night TV, this is around the time that programmes such as *Strictly Come Dancing* begin again. A couple of months later around November we are blessed with *I'm a Celebrity Get Me Out of Here* (that's when you know Christmas is nearly here!). But if you aren't a fan of glitzy dancing, or celebrities eating bugs, then you can make your own version of Saturday night entertainment. My sister and I had been planning a "spooky night" for a few weeks. I really wanted to watch the film *Practical Magic* (which is both my sister and my mam's favourite film) so we set a night aside when we both finished work and I came over to her house to watch it.

I brought over my Halloween Mickey blanket and pyjamas to stay the night. My sister had put cinnamon whirls in the oven ready for when I arrived. Her whole house smelt like a bakery; it was heavenly. She did her bedtime routine with my niece and then once she was asleep, we ordered an Indian takeaway and stuck the film on. The takeaway finally arrived (smelling fantastic) and we settled in. In case you're wondering what I ordered; I had an onion bhaji and mint yoghurt for starters and then half masala, half butter chicken, garlic chips, garlic naan and pilau rice. Just to make your mouth water! I have to admit, my eyes were definitely bigger than my stomach!

I'm going to give it to my sister, she is an excellent host. She had lots of delicious smelling autumnal candles dotted about, and a set of pumpkin fairy lights under her TV which made the whole room glow orange. It's the little things like this that really set the mood. Keep these things in mind if you're planning on recreating our night! We had our cinnamon whirls on a ghost plate I had bought from B&M and popcorn in pumpkin bowls. Once I had my blanket on I was nearly ready to fall asleep then and there!

The film itself was so perfectly **witchy**. It's a classic film that is watched during spooky season by Halloween lovers, like me. Starring absolute icons Sandra Bullock, Nicole Kidman, Stockard Channing and Dianne West. It's based on the book by Alice Hoffman, about the Owens sisters who are doomed by a family curse that any man they fall in love with will die. It's tragic, funny, and quirky. The soundtrack is also absolute perfection with several songs from Stevie Nicks, my favourite musical witch! I fell in love with the Owens family, particularly the relationship between the two sisters and their two aunties. I mean, who doesn't want a pair of witchy aunties?! They concocted potions, cast spells, drank midnight margaritas, and danced the night away. The margaritas scene was actually my favourite scene of the film. Apparently, one of the actresses had bought some cheap tequila, and they ended up actually getting drunk during that scene!

It was a very cosy night. If you're ever feeling like you need a bit of self-care or want to spend time with a family member then I would definitely suggest doing something similar to this. You could change the film and watch something else e.g., watch episodes of a spooky TV show like American Horror Story or Supernatural. Get in your favourite takeaway e.g., pizza, Chinese, Indian etc, have some autumnal snacks and drinks on the side, wrap up in fluffy blankets and switch your mind off for a bit! It's a night in that doesn't require too much planning or prep, but still feels like it goes with the theme.

The Nun (21st September 2018)

Cinema trip with family

This actually came up recently in my Snapchat memories and I couldn't resist placing it in here! In 2018 I went to the cinema with my two cousins, my cousin's best friend and my two aunties. We stupidly decided to go see *The Nun* which at the time, was the latest instalment in *The Conjuring* universe. At this time, little ole 21-year-old me was **terrified** of horror films. I think, ironically, the only horror films that I braved in the cinema were the *Annabelle* films, also part of The Conjuring series. What on earth was I thinking.

I remember putting on my best autumnal outfit which consisted of a cream jumper with a tartan collar, a black skirt, tights, and boots. I put on my cute *Coraline* necklace (which sadly broke a while ago) and was ready to go to the cinema! We got there and purchased some snacks, I remember buying a milkshake, either Oreo or Crunchie flavoured (delicious) and we sat down in our seats ready to watch.

It...was...terrifying. The Nun herself continues to haunt my nightmares to this day, even though the actress was in *The Princess Diaries*. I remember singing the Genovian national anthem to myself when the really scary scenes were on screen to calm myself down. The film also starred Taissa Farmiga, who played Violet in AHS Murder House and Zoe in AHS Coven. Fun fact: I share a birthday with her! Anyway, the film was set against the backdrop of Italy, in the Vatican. I loved the use of history in this film.

The film had this booming, haunting score whenever the Nun was either present or being a creeper and it absolutely petrified me whenever it happened. I remember at some point in the film there was a jump scare and it was very random. So random that none of us saw it coming and we all jumped out of our skins, including my aunties. We could not hold in the laughter as it was so funny. Maybe not the right time but it was too hilarious not to laugh at. These are always the best parts of horror films. When things break the tension.

National Ghost Hunting Day (30th September)

"I ain't afraid of no ghost!"

Ghostbusters, 1984

Happy National Ghost Hunting Day! I told you there was a day for everything! This day commemorates the practice of "ghost hunting". Now, for being the spooky girl that I say that I am, I've never actually been ghost-hunting before! You could say there's a few kinds of ghost-hunting. You have the amateur social media ghost-hunting that a lot of Youtubers document. They explore various supposedly haunted locations, with their vlogging camera and maybe an EVP machine or a spirit box that they've got off Amazon (no shade!). Then you have the official ghost-hunters that film for high profile TV shows that have a full team with professional equipment etc. I suppose you could class playing with Ouija boards and seances as "ghost-hunting" as they're trying to get into contact with spirits from beyond the grave. In ghost-hunting sessions, sometimes they'll use a Ouija board to try and speak to the ghost in question, but a lot of the time they rely on spirit boxes, EMF readers etc.

Mystic Meg: the Play

When I was studying GCSE Drama in school we got to write, create, and perform our own play (one of the best projects I've ever done) as part of our studies. The group that I was working with, we decided to write a play about ghosts, because for some reason we were all really obsessed with ghosts, goodness knows why... The story took form in the shape of a group of friends who one day are bored and decide to play around with a Ouija board (not recommended) and accidentally summon a demon, not a friendly spirit. After the event they all start to experience forms of paranormal activity. So, they decide to go to the Hoppings and visit a kooky psychic/spirit medium named Mystic Meg (played by moi) who performs a crazy séance to try and get rid of the spirit, only to realise that it has possessed one of the friends without them realising...

I remember performing this play in front of our Drama class and feeling such a **buzz** off of getting an applause. I can't actually remember what the play was graded as (definitely an A*!) but playing the character of Mystic Meg was just thrilling. I really let loose and took on this character of the crazy medium. Someone in my class actually told me for one assignment that I came across as having the same energy of a CBeebies presenter, which I definitely take as a compliment! Wanting to ghost-hunt and dabble in the paranormal world was deep-rooted in high school, and who knows? I might dig the play back out and rewrite it...

Ghost-Hunting on YouTube

Amateur as it may be, I love watching ghost-hunting on YouTube. Normally they're able to edit it into something fun, but also suspenseful so you feel like it's not as scary as it seems. Ghost-hunting can be fun for all the family! I don't know if I could ever personally go ghost-hunting, but I can live through it through these channels and videos. I'm going to list some of my favourite ghost-hunting series that I've come across on YouTube that you may also like.

Glam and Gore

I've watched Mykie from *Glam and Gore* for a few years. My older sister introduced me to her during when she was participating in the "FACE Awards". As her channel suggests, she does glam make-up and gory special effects make-up. She's a loveable weirdo and a spooky beauty queen. She also does ghost-hunting. Quite a few actually! Her first ghost-hunting series was "Ghost-Hunting for Halloween" where she did special effects make-up in a certain haunted location e.g. Jerome Arizona, the Queen Mary (haunted ship), the Hollywood Rosevelt (haunted hotel), Sleepy Hollow etc. The looks were all themed with the location, e.g. Ursula on the Queen Mary, a witch in Sleepy Hollow, Marilyn Monroe in the Hollywood Rosevelt (she's said to haunt that exact hotel).

She then did a revival of the ghost-hunting but going to more locations including Salem, the Lizzie Borden House, Hotel Monte Vista, Chateau Marmont etc. In these videos she had "the squad" helping with the hunting e.g. her boyfriend, her camera man, more friends etc. Although I like the ghost-hunting with the make-up looks, I liked seeing more of the friendship group, because they were able to bounce off of each other when the "spooky stuff" is happening. One other thing I love about Mykie is that she really researches and respects the places that she visits, when a lot of people don't and will blindly stumble into a place without knowing the history.

Garrett Watts

Originally Garrett was associated with another Youtuber and did ghost-hunting with them, but then he branched out and started doing his own ghost-hunting adventures, which are actually titled in a playlist as "Haunted Adventures". I love Garrett anyway, from watching him in other Youtuber's videos. His quirky energy always made me smile, so seeing his own videos were even better!

In his "Haunted Adventures" he hunts in an apartment, hotel, ice-cream shop, make-up studio, Victorian Mansion etc. All of these he does with his camera man and friend, Andrew, who also starred in other Youtuber's ghost-hunting series. A lot of these are actually quite meaty videos, a couple being over 2 hours long, like a film! Again, mixed with a dash of humour and some spooky suspense it makes up for a great series!

Hocus Pocus 2 release (30th September 2022)

"Sistaaaaaahhhs!" The time has finally come. Don your emerald capes, grab your broomsticks, grab a child to suck the life out of, because it's time for the release of *Hocus Pocus 2*! Ever since they announced that they were making a sequel, I have been waiting and waiting. *Hocus Pocus* has been my favourite Halloween film since I was tiny. I watched it even

when it wasn't Halloween. The idea that they were doing a sequel nearly 30 years later was incredibly exciting, but also made me nervous. Would it have the same level of nostalgia as it did when I was a child? Or will it surpass my expectations completely? Only time would tell...

Flash forward to the date you see before you: 30th September 2022. I had been at work all day but when I got home I was getting changed straight away and heading to my sister's house where we were having a "Hocus Pocus 2: watch party" with our cousins. My sister actually bought us all matching autumnal Starbucks coffee cups with our names written on, so we could have hot chocolate or pumpkin spice lattes. I made a spooky cheeseboard (even trying to replicate the cheese graveyard that I mentioned earlier!) and my other cousin brought a Halloween Millie's Cookie for us to share. Once we had all of our snack plates ready, it was time to watch the film!

The review:

I personally **loved** the film. We had some scenes at the beginning of the film that took place with the Sanderson Sisters as children in Salem. The actresses that were chosen to play them were absolutely spot-on, down to each of the sisters' quirky mannerisms. The actual story took place in modern-day Salem with two baby Gen-Z witches who accidentally bring the Sanderson Sisters back to life after lighting the Black Flame Candle again. You would think people would have learnt after last time?! The film actually has a different storyline from the novel *Hocus Pocus and the All-New Sequel* which came out a few years beforehand. That book took the daughter of Max and Allison Dennison and had her having a run in with the three iconic witches. Although I would have loved to see Max and Allison as parents on the big screen (maybe *Hocus Pocus 3???)* I liked having the Gen Z teens as the protagonists of this film. We also had a reappearance from Billy Butcherson, Winnie's zombified ex-boyfriend. His make-up wasn't exactly the same as the original, but it was nearly 30 years later so they did a great job! This was the perfect cozy night with great vibes and some wicked witchery thrown in...

Autumnween: October (Black Cat Awareness Month)

"This is Halloween, this is Halloween, pumpkins scream in the dead of night. This is Halloween everybody make a scene. Trick or treat til' the neighbours gonna die of fright!"

Halloween Town Chorus, The Nightmare Before Christmas.

Eek! This is it! As Anne Shirley (of Green Gables) once said, "I'm so glad I live in a world where there are Octobers". All the leaves are brown, and the sky is grey. Yes, those are lyrics from *California Dreaming* by the Beach Boys. Although the song actually talks about a winter's day, I feel like it's more suited to an autumn day. Who doesn't love going on a brisk walk on an autumn day? Wrapping up warm in a woollen scarf (my colour preference is red with black checks), adorning an oversized coat and a bobble hat. Walking through crunchy leaves with a hot drink in your hand. Life couldn't get any better than that!

Although Halloween is every creep's end goal, I want to discuss the beauty of Autumn also. October will be filled with all of the whimsy of the season. The witchy ways of the season. Sometimes I feel like the build-up to the celebration is even more fun than the actual day. I'll also be sharing the ways I've celebrated Halloween in recent years, so grab yourself a hot drink and tuck into this cozy section!

International Coffee Day (1ˢᵗ October)

"Get in bitches, we're going to get Pumpkin Spice Lattes!" review.

You've heard it here first folks, it's officially Pumpkin Spice Latte season! Those lucky Americans always get them a little earlier than we do but honestly, it's better late than never! Coffee shops begin to bring out their autumnal drinks menus which makes my little pumpkin orange heart sing! Whether you're out with a friend, or taking yourself on a solo coffee date, there's a coffee out there for you! Below you will find some little reviews of some autumnal coffees that I have tried throughout the months of September and October!

Pumpkin Spice crème Frappuccino (Starbucks) 3rd September: I tried this on a breakfast date with my sister and niece before heading to a rubber duck race! It tasted like a nice-smelling candle (please don't eat candles!) and it was very orange, so perfect for the season.

Maple Hazel Iced Latte (Costa) 13th September: This drink was very sweet, and you could really taste the maple syrup in it! Had this on a lovely day out with family.

Salted Caramel Iced Frappuccino (Black Sheep Coffee) 3rd October: I had an afternoon off from work, so I popped into town and took myself on a solo coffee date! This was a very sweet drink, not necessarily autumnal but still delicious.

Wednesday Vanilla and Blueberry Bubble tea (Bubble Ci-Tea) 18th October: This was part of a "Nevermore" themed drinks menu and considering I've only ever had bubble tea once; this was absolutely lush! Vanilla and blueberry is such a heavenly flavour combination, and I bought a Wednesday Bubble Tea pin!

Pumpkin Spice Espresso Martini (Boulevard NCL) 21st October: Bit tipsy on a night out with my friend seeing a Halloween drag show (yes, and it was amazing!) so I went a bit wild on the Halloween-themed drinks menu. Was this disgusting? Yes. Did I keep drinking it? Of course I did!

Ghost Pumpkin Frappuccino (Starbucks) 25th October: The last autumnal drink I managed to squeeze in before the end of October. It was very sweet and tasted like blue raspberry!

National Mushroom Day (15ᵗʰ October)

We've had National Mushroom month (September) now it's time for National Mushroom Day! As I said earlier, my interest in mushrooms emerged in Autumn 2022, when I noticed lots of mushrooms growing around my workplace. Now, I still don't know if it was because I just wasn't paying attention, but I noticed so many after that!

There're so many reasons why I'm so fascinated by them. I love the way they sprout from the ground, and then sink back into the ground when no one is watching. They are such funny little things; their appearances are so odd but captivating! I also love how you can find them in every season, I used to think they were only Autumn beings but turns out they appear all year round! As it stands I've managed to find mushrooms in every season.

For celebrating this day, you could try your hand at mushroom hunting! Now I am not an expert and I'm still learning about the different types of mushrooms, which ones are edible, and which are poisonous. Don't worry, if I see any out and about I never touch them and only take photos. I've also been discussing this with the children in my nursery as we've spotted a few small mushrooms in our play area and I always talk safety precautions first with them, warning that we can't touch but we can look and take pictures.

If you are an experienced mushroom forager then I would use this day to go on a celebratory forage. Whatever you find you can use to cook your favourite mushroom meal (if you find edible species) or even create art! If you are a beginner in "Mycology" (study of fungi) then I suggest doing some research, if you do find any out and about (remember, you don't need to delve into the depths of the ancient forest to find them!) you could take a moment and sketch them, or even use chalks or paint to colour them in. Or if you're a *'big spender'* like me, then you could look online for some cute mushroom related items such as prints, bookmarks, mugs, even clothes!

National Pasta Day (17th October)

In 2022 Aldi released Halloween-shaped pasta. Yes, you heard that right! As a person who is a sucker for anything Halloween themed, I had to buy them. In fact, I bought five bags! The bags were only small so you could say I was just stocking up. Pasta just so happens to be one of my favourite dishes (Pasta carbonara and bolognaise to be specific!) so this day is right up my alley! If you are also a lover of pasta and Halloween you could quite simply use that and make your favourite pasta dish to enjoy. It doesn't have to be Halloween-shaped, but I have seen black and white striped pasta bows (Farfalline Magia Bianca, also known as Black and White Zebra Bowties), black spaghetti etc.

I have to say, my Mam makes the best pasta bolognaise. She's made it since I was a kid, and it was one of my favourite childhood meals. I prefer fusilli pasta with my bolognaise, and a mountain of cheese on top. Now, my Mam has very kindly donated her recipe to this book so that I can share it with all of you! I hope you enjoy your putrid pastas!

Pasta Bolognaise recipe (by Lynn Scott)

1. **Take a large carrot, celery sticks (both chopped), grated carrots and smoked bacon and fry it together.**
2. **Add beef/steak mine and 'brown it'.**
3. **Add oregano to taste and a beef stock cube.**
4. **Add two-three tins of tomatoes and simmer.**
5. **Add chopped mushrooms.**
6. **Serve up with your choice of base e.g. Halloween-shaped pasta, chips, tortilla crisps etc.**
7. **Sprinkle on your choice of cheese. Don't scrimp on the cheddar!**

National Candy Corn Day (30th October)

We actually do not have this "candy" in the UK! If you are American and reading this (Hiya!) then you already know what it is, and apparently dislike it. Candy Corn is a bit like Marmite I think, you either love it or hate it. It's basically a pyramid-shaped sweet divided into three different colours: yellow, white and orange. It apparently has a waxy texture, and the flavours are based on honey, vanilla, butter and sugar.

Candy Corn was invented in the 1800s by candymaker George Renninger. Apparently Candy Corn isn't even the sweet's original name! It used to be called "Chicken Feed" with colourful roosters illustrating the packaging. I feel like its newer name suits it better. There are so many different types of Candy Corn that they bring it out for Christmas, Valentine's Day, even Thanksgiving!

Even though it is apparently a very popular Halloween candy, we do not have it here, unless you order it online. If you can't get your hands on the sweet treat you can still celebrate the day by wearing yellow, white and orange or eating your favourite Halloween sweets. In a British child's trick or treat bag, you are more likely to come across sweets such as Smarties, Drumstick lollies, mini-Snickers and Mars Bars, chocolate eyeballs, Animal Bars, mini–Milky Ways, Flump marshmallows etc. Flumps in particular were always my favourite Halloween sweet, as well as ghost-shaped marshmallows!

National Magic Day and Halloween (31st October)

Happy Halloween everyone! The spookiest night of the year is finally here. If Halloween lands on a weekday, I'm normally at work, which involves me doing my usual work routine with the children. We like to have Halloween activities set up to do with them and they adorably come in dressed in costume. Then it's back home for tea and answering the door to trick or treaters. Oh, how times have changed! Being in your twenties is strange, looking at the kids on your doorstep dressed as vampires and ghouls, and realising that it wasn't too long ago that *you* were doing the same thing as them. Gobbling down your potato smiley faces and beans hurriedly while your Mam cuts the holes out of a bin bag for your 'witch' costume. Rushing some Halloween make-up so that you can get out there and find those sweets! The excitement was real.

Obviously as an adult it isn't as socially acceptable to trick or treat anymore. If you want to though than don't listen to what anyone thinks and get out and do it! But there are so many other ways to celebrate Halloween. I feel like Halloween night always goes way too quickly. If you're like me and work 9-5 then you probably won't have time to celebrate during the day, but once you get home, light a pumpkin candle, and stick on your favourite horror movie! When I was younger, channels like CITV, CBBC and the Disney Channel would air Halloween specials of their TV shows and I used to spend my night watching them with a hot chocolate. I would also sometimes help my Mam hand out sweets to the trick or treaters and melt at all of the adorable costumes.

If Halloween lands on a Friday or the weekend, then you might go to a Halloween party, a spooky event or have a movie night with friends. Whichever way you choose to commemorate, make sure you have fun! I don't have many suggestions for Halloween night, but I did want to show some other ways that I've celebrated throughout the month, because sometimes, the build-up can just as exciting as the actual day! In 2022 I did a few different Halloween activities throughout the month. I don't think I've ever done so many different excursions in one month before! It was nice to experience Halloween in alternative forms.

Halloween activities:

Throughout the month of October, I like to do different activities out of the house. If you don't want to spend money then that is totally up to you and there are plenty of cheap and easy ways to celebrate Halloween at home! Here are the activities that I did in 2022.

Pumpkin Picking

Up until about 3 years ago I didn't even realise that pumpkin picking existed in the UK! Typically, pumpkin patches only exist in America, in massive patches with hayrides, corn mazes, rides, photo opportunities etc, like mini autumnal fairgrounds! However, if you go pumpkin picking in the UK, our patches are grown on farms where you normally go to walk around the farm shops for fresh fruit and vegetables. A lot of them put out quirky photo set-ups so you can take photos, have mini funfairs on, and then after you've picked your pumpkins you can retreat to the comforting warmth of the farm café for a hot chocolate and a cake or two!

The first time I went picking for pumpkins was 2 years ago in 2021, with my sisters and my niece. I was so excited! I brought my favourite graphic novel *Pumpkinheads* by Rainbow Rowell to take photos against the orange and green backdrop of the patch and wore an outfit adorned with pumpkins. My niece was 8 months old and seeing her all dressed in her woolly pumpkin hat that my Mam knitted for her was the sweetest thing.

One of my favourite things about Pumpkin Picking each year has been watching my niece grow and develop and begin to understand it more. Obviously in her first year she couldn't walk yet so my sister had her in a papoose to carry her around. In her second year she could walk and had more awareness of what was going on around her, so she was able to walk around and point at different pumpkins.

Unfortunately, this year (2023) I haven't been able to go Pumpkin Picking. I know! So much sadness (joking). The weather has been extremely bad with long periods of rainfall. The rain turned the pumpkin patch into a giant muddy puddle. At one point it was so bad that whole sections were cordoned off and you could only walk in one area! I think we just picked the wrong day to go on. So next year, we know to be more prepared. However, that hasn't turned me off going Pumpkin Picking and I still want to continue for as long as they exist!

Hocus Pocus Afternoon Tea

My Mam and I absolutely adore afternoon tea. I've discussed this earlier on in the book about afternoon tea and the joys of picnics. However, I had never had a Halloween afternoon tea! I saw that The Great British Cupcakery that we have in Newcastle was hosting Hocus Pocus themed afternoon teas in October. I straight away booked tickets for me and my Mam to go as we are both afternoon tea enthusiasts.

The Great British Cupcakery is pastel heaven. It has candyfloss pink walls, the most delectable cakes and pastries behind a glass case, and a flower wall with the café's logo on it (great for photos!). We headed down during the October half term to see what it was all about. We both ordered two unicorn pink hot chocolates (with spooky sprinkles) and our afternoon tea set which consisted of a selection of sandwiches, scones, and the most scrumptious cakes, we were so full off of two sandwiches and one cake!

Slasher Villian Photoshoot

I don't think I've ever laughed so much in one night. A few months beforehand, when our DnD party started organising our sessions, I had the idea to meet up for Halloween and play DnD in costume. We went with a Horror Villian theme and pulled names out of a bowl to decide who was going to be who. I ended up with... Micheal Myers! Now I was at a huge advantage because I already owned a blue jumpsuit (it was for work during the pandemic...) and all I needed was a Micheal Myers mask which I think my sister ordered for me off the internet. When it arrived, my gosh, it was the scariest mask I've ever seen.

The other members of our party were Freddy Krueger, Ghostface and Jason Voorhees. Basically, the main horror "crew". After we took lots of photos, some TikTok's and played the actual DnD session, we decided to go for a spooky walk, as my cousin lives in a small village with a couple of graveyards. If anyone had come across us in the night they would have thought that they were nuts! And I suppose we are! After we took some more photos by torchlight on an incredibly creepy path leading into some ominous-looking woods and scaring ourselves by every snap of a twig or whistle of the wind, we decided to go act even more nuts by going to the local park and playing on the swings. Bearing in mind we are all in our 20s... you only live once!

Pumpkin Flower Arranging

If you aren't a fan of pumpkin carving, there are alternative activities that you can try! Me and my sister went to a "pumpkin flower arranging" class at her brother-in-law's restaurant. The aim was to hollow out a pumpkin and use the pumpkin as a 'plant pot' with an arrangement of autumnal flowers sticking out. This activity was very hands-on and practical, so if you enjoy doing practical activities then it will definitely be up your street!

There were a few different steps to create your pumpkin flowerpot. It involved cutting out and carving out your pumpkin, putting a block of special kind of solid foam (which I cannot for the life of me remember the name of!) and pushing in your flowers with sticks to keep them in line. It was certainly something I've never done before, so it was nice to try something new! Along with the class we also got a pizza (I went with Chicken Kiev) and a glass of fizz!

More Halloween activities:

Boo Basket: This is a fairly new thing I've seen floating around the internet, but people have been creating "boo baskets" for their significant others, friends, or family. You get a basket (you can find them in most homeware sections in shops) even better if it's a Halloween colour e.g. orange or black, line it with a fluffy blanket or a fleecy throw, and fill it with autumnal/Halloween products that you know the recipient will enjoy e.g. a pumpkin spice candle or autumnal wax melts, sachets of coffee or hot chocolate, Halloween sweets, a spooky book etc. My love language is gifts, so if anyone did this for me, I would marry them! This is not only a cute gift, but hunting for the presents to go in the basket can also be fun, like Halloween hunting in October!

Boo Bath: I actually did this for a TikTok in October 2021, and it was so much fun to create! It was another "trend" I'd seen floating around, more directed towards mams making them for their kids, but I had to jump on the trend as well. I ran myself a hot bath and used the "Bat Art" bath bomb from the Lush Halloween collection. It's a black sparkly bath bomb in the shape of a bat, which turned the water a gorgeous purple-black colour. I then chucked in some cracked glow sticks, some plastic skeletons and bats, and glow-in-the-dark spiders. Turn your bathroom lights off and it's like lightshow in your bath! You can add to this further by making yourself a spooky cocktail or soft drink and bask in the mood lighting. I would move the skeletons out of the way before you sit in it though, you don't want to sit on a skeleton hand!

Fall "Yes" Day: I actually saw an American couple do this on Instagram and thought it was such a cute date idea! You could even do this with a friend or even a sibling. In America I've mentioned that they do fall/Halloween way better than the UK do. So, in the video, the woman's husband said "yes" to everything that she asked to do, e.g. a day of 'fall' excursions! They went to get pumpkin spice lattes, they went to get fall decorations from Hobby Lobby, which I think is like the American version of Hobby Craft. They went to a restaurant called Panera and ordered hot soup and bread, and lastly to TJ Maxx (TK Maxx in the UK) to get a 'fall outfit'. Now I think this is a pretty solid day out! It's a bit trickier to do in the UK, but if you do it in October then there will definitely be more options for you to do. For example, you could definitely go to Starbucks and get a pumpkin spice latte or any of their autumnal drinks, or alternatively Costa normally release an autumn menu as well. You could go to TK Maxx/HomeSense to get Halloween decorations, if there's any horror films out at the time you could go to the cinema and watch one or have a chilled night watching any spooky on Netflix! Inspiration from: @hannahandregal

Boo Dinner: I've seen many people do "Disney dinners" where they have a movie night in, with a menu of food inspired by a certain Disney film. I've also seen a girl do a "Boo Dinner" where she had a themed menu of *Beetlejuice* foods and watched the film with her girlfriend for the anniversary of *Beetlejuice*. One of the best creepy films with a delicious menu that you can recreate is definitely *Coraline*. Having a night in with a *Coraline* dinner, consisting of roast chicken, corn on the cob, mashed potatoes, gravy, cherry chocolate cupcakes, a "Welcome Home" cake and mango milkshakes sounds like the cosiest night in! If you didn't think the food from *Coraline* didn't look delicious, you are lying to yourself! To be fair, the *Coraline* dinner is basically a British Sunday Roast, so it doesn't seem too complicated to make!

Horror Film Anniversaries: In 2023 we had quite a few big spooky film anniversaries! I love a good film anniversary because it gives me the opportunity to watch the film for nostalgic purposes. Although not all of these actually released during spooky season, here's a list of some anniversaries to keep your eye out for!

- Hocus Pocus 30th Anniversary- 29th October (1993)

- Halloweentown 25th Anniversary- 17th October (1998)
- Beetlejuice 35th Anniversary-30th March (1988)
- Practical Magic 25th Anniversary-16th October (1998)
- The Exorcist 50th Anniversary- 26th December (1973)
- Halloween 45th Anniversary-25th October (1978)
- Ernest Scared Stupid- 11th October (1991)

Autumnween: November

I used to think that as soon as Halloween ended, Christmas began. How wrong I was! I genuinely didn't realise that Autumn didn't end until mid-December. I know it sounds silly but that's what I thought! Now I know that we have another beautiful month of Autumn to live through. Again, I used to forget about November. It was a "filler month" that didn't mean anything to me. But now, I see November for all its loveliness. The frosty air, the sleeting rain, the darker nights. It's like Mother Nature has dimmed the sitting room lights, so that you're just sitting in a low orange glow. The stars are so much brighter in the sky, the air feels cleaner and crisper.

November is the perfect time to curl up in an armchair, pull a knitted blanket over you and get lost in a gloomy ghost story or a murder mystery. Darling Desi also recommended watching black and white films and playing board games such as Cluedo. Basically, November is peak-cosy month before the madness of Christmas begins! As much as I love Christmas I have to admit that it does get very hectic what with seeing family, going to Christmas markets, buying presents etc. November reminds us that it's okay to slow down for a minute, take a deep breath and soak in our surroundings.

If you're American, November equals Thanksgiving season. We don't actually celebrate that in the UK, but we do have a few of our own celebrations that we take part in. The first is of course Bonfire Night on the 5th of November, the second is Remembrance Sunday on the 12th of November and the third is

Children in Need which takes place on the 17[th of] November. If I've missed any out I do apologise! I know "Day of the Dead" is on the 2nd of November, which is definitely a spooky day for sure! But whatever you celebrate I hope you have the best time. You don't need to fit everything into your schedule in November. If all you want to do is cozy up and read, do that!

Bonfire/Guy Fawkes Night (5th November)

"Remember, remember the fifth of November,
Gunpowder treason and plot.
I know of no reason why the Gunpowder treason
Should ever be forgot.

Ahh, the age-old story of Guy Fawkes threatening to blow up Parliament... there's nothing scarier than that! Us Brits enjoy celebrating the strange and macabre, so we turned a plot to use explosives on rich people into a fun, family friendly event! Usually near the end of October, and sometimes earlier, you'll be having your nightly Netflix series binge, when that dreaded sound of fireworks explodes off in the distance. You'll roll your eyes and think, it's already begun. From the 31st of October, the fireworks get more frequent as the nights go on. They thankfully stop after the 5th of November but there's always some nutter still setting them off, especially if you live in a rough area.

Guy Fawkes Night, or Bonfire Night as it's more commonly referred to as involves you wrapping up in a winter coat (because it's finally getting cold *ahem, looking at you 2023 September-October offensive heatwave! * And heading out to a muddy field. You will stand in this crowded muddy field in a hat, scarf, and coat, paying ridiculous prices for a hot dog or a Styrofoam cup of soup and watch colourful fireworks exploding in the night sky above you. It does end up being a nice night to be fair, but it probably seems very strange to someone whose never celebrated it.

My childhood memories of Bonfire Night include going to my primary school's Bonfire Display in the school yard, drinking hot chocolate with my friends. Or my dad would set off little rockets in our back garden to watch, and we'd have sparklers (absolute death traps) to play with, twirling them around like fairy wands. Also, one year we went to a family member's house for their fireworks display, and my Mam was dishing out hot tomato soup for everyone when she accidentally spilt it on her hand, and so the saga of "the Blister on Mam's hand" began...

International Clown Day (5ᵗʰ November)

"BEEP, BEEP, Richie!"

IT miniseries (1990)

Now I know not everyone is a fan of clowns. For me, I'm indifferent. I think they're creepy, and not particularly funny, but they don't massively scare me. I say that but if a clown knocked on my bedroom door right now I would probably faint. Wait... what's that noise? I better go check what it is. It's- oh my god, what is that!!!..............................

Greetings, it's Bobbins the Clown! I've actually ate Megan (she was particularly tasty!) so she unfortunately can't continue writing this section. Not that it was any good anyways, but now I'm here, it'll be so much better! I'm here to tell you how to celebrate the best day of the year... INTERNATIONAL CLOWN DAY!!!

Watch clown films. Unless you're a wuss, but my favourites include Killer Clowns from Outer Space, IT (the new ones and the miniseries (Tim Curry really is a legend!), The Terrifier, House of 1000 Corpses etc.

*Attempt a clownish make up look. Unless you're that ugly that you might crack your mirror, in that case I wouldn't bother! *Blows raspberry**

Read clown books, like Clown in a Cornfield or Cotton Candy Massacre. Try not to die of boredom while reading!

Eat candyfloss or make a fairground themed snack. We clown love food. And children. We like eating children. Lots of them...

*You know, I think I'm regretting eating that girl. She's making my belly feel really. Really.. oh god.........*burps*................................*

Sorry, what just happened? Shall we, erm- continue onto the next section? That was really weird...

Stranger Things Day (6th November)

6th November 1983... in 2022 it had technically been "39 years" since Will Byers was snatched by the Demogorgon and absorbed into the Upside Down in the TV show. It's strange to think that now Will, Mike, Dustin, Lucas, El and Max would be in their 40s or 50s (I'm not the best at Maths). At this current moment they've started filming the last season, Season 5. I'm not quite ready to let it go, just yet. It's been such a wild ride since Season 1, and it's had a massive shift in pop culture.

In my late teenage years, I became obsessed with 80s films, like the Brat Pack films, anything with River Phoenix (I watched *Stand by Me* so many times!) etc. But since I was a kid I loved *The Goonies, The Lost Boys, The Labyrinth, Teen Wolf* etc. I feel like since *Stranger Things* first premiered there's been a resurgence of 80s style films, and 'supernatural kid adventures' similar to *The Goonies, Monster Squad, Never-ending Story, Explorers, ET* etc. And books as well e.g. *My Best Friend's Exorcism, Clown in a Cornfield, Dead Flip* to name a few!

When I started watching *Stranger Things* it immediately drew me in, as I said because it was so similar to the things that I loved watching as a child. There are so many parallels to them as well, like I said earlier the train tracks from *Stand by Me*, even dressing a clueless El up like the loveable alien ET. There's also a lot of parallels to Stephen King, especially his novel and miniseries *IT*. The 'new' IT movies (the first one came out in 2017) actually changed the time period, as in the miniseries it was set in the 1950s, and they changed it to the 1980s to go with the change in pop culture, as *Stranger Things* came out in 2016, just 1 year before!

So, since it is "Stranger Things Day" you can of course celebrate it in any way you like, I've already spoken about some *Stranger Things* activities that you can do. I'll not repeat all of them but here's some other ways you can celebrate this special day!

- Rewatch (or watch for the first time) all the seasons. Set a day aside for yourself, put on some comfy clothes, make a hot drink (remember, it's still November!) and lose yourself in Hawkins, Indiana...
- Make your own "Eggo Waffles". We don't actually have Eggos (El's favourite snack) in the UK. But we do have normal waffles that you can get in most supermarkets. Grab a pack, toast some, drizzle with maple syrup, honey, or dessert sauce, and sprinkle some Smarties on and enjoy!
- Draw your favourite character. If you're artistic or not, trying to draw your favourite character from the show can be super fun! Colour it in or even paint if you're feeling like Bob Ross!
- Read a *Stranger Things* book. There's been a few official books released from the 'multiverse' of ST, but also you can have a hunt for books that have the same vibes such as *Dead Flip*.

- Go for a "Hot Demogorgon Walk" (like a Hot Girl Walk) and listen to the soundtrack. The show has some absolutely beautiful music and some cracking 80s songs, so take yourself on a little walk and immerse yourself through sound. My favourite piece of music is the epic version of *Separate Ways (Worlds Apart)* by Journey from Season 4.

Wednesday release Day (23rd November 2022)

Ever since Netflix announced that we were getting a TV show all about our favourite alternative Goth Girl with a sharp wit, I was all about it. I grew up with the 90s live action adaptations, with *The Addams Family* being released in 1991, and *The Addams Family Values* released in 1993. Both came out before I was born but both films grew a "cult following" that lined up with the outpouring of love for the OG Charles Addams comic. Before the 90s films we also had the black-and-white TV series released in 1964 to 1966, *The Addams Family* and *The Addams Family Fun House* both released in 1973, one a cartoon adaptation of the live action series and the other a musical variety show pilot that didn't do as well as they would have hoped. We then had *Halloween with the New Addams Family* in 1977, a made-for-TV seasonal special with a few of the original cast members from the 60s TV show. *The Addams Family: the Animated Series* from 1992-1993, then the two 90s films I spoke about earlier, followed by *The New Addams Family* from 1998-1999, a Canadian remake of the original show, then *The Addams Family Reunion* in 1998, a direct to video film made as a reboot of the earlier 90s films. It wasn't until years later (2019-2022) that we got two new animated *Addams Family* films and the highly anticipated *Wednesday* show.

It seemed like the 90s were desperate to keep the spirit of Hollywood's most macabre family (only slightly beating them with creepiness by *the Munster's*?) alive and kicking. Personally, my favourite adaptations were the 90s films that I've mentioned. It wasn't just for Raul Julia as Gomez, Angelica

Houston as Morticia, Christina Ricci as Wednesday (although she absolutely **slayed** in the role!) or even Christopher Lloyd as bumbling Uncle Fester. There's a quirkiness about the films that the other reboots haven't quite touched on. It helps that we introduced to the absolute legend that is Debbie in *The Addams Family Values*. *"I mean really Debbie... pastels?"* is a crime only the Addams clan would think is worse than murder itself. It's curious to see how old people are or what generation they come from by which *Addams Family* adaptation they remember watching. I'm a 90s baby so I obviously watched those films, but my parents are both "boomers" and they used to watch the 1960s TV show. Even now there's animated films for Generation Alpha, and the Netflix's *Wednesday* is definitely geared towards Gen Z, with a few nostalgic 90s kids thrown into the audience.

Netflix's Wednesday

In the very early stages of promo for Wednesday, it was advertised as a "supernatural murder mystery" which intrigued me immediately. From 2020 onwards I fell in love with the true crime/horror/thriller's genre in both films and books. So, anything that was categorised as a 'murder mystery' I was all in for. I also loved listening to true crime YouTube channels and later podcasts. I'm actually listening to a true crime episode as I'm writing this! Wednesday would definitely be proud...

The premise of Wednesday was about a teenage Wednesday Addams, who recently started experiencing psychic visions which she didn't wish to share with anyone. Wednesday is just as dark and cynical as she always has been, with a splash of teenage angst. After an incident that Wednesday causes at her high school, she is shipped off to Nevermore Academy, a boarding school for outcasts and misfit's aka monsters. This academy is also where her parents both went to school, which makes it so much more insufferable for Wednesday. When she arrives, she gets tangled up in a murder mystery surrounding the school's history and is determined to solve it, no matter the cost.

One thing that I haven't actually mentioned about this adaptation is that it was actually directed by Tim Burton. Yes, **the Tim Burton** who created *Edward Scissorhands*, *Beetlejuice*, *Sweeney Todd* etc. You can't get spookier than this guy! The show is so rooted in Burton's vibes from the pale colour palette, the academy inspired by Edgar Allan Poe, monstrous shenanigans etc. The show has such a cool and creepy vibe that I was immediately sucked in. Wednesday becomes a bit of teenage detective during solving this case, reminding me very much of Pip Fitz-Amobi from *A Good Girl's Guide to Murder* (my favourite book trilogy!). Wednesday doesn't let anyone influence her crime-solving, despite many warnings and deterring from various characters. In the series Wednesday is also presented as being a writer, writing a book very similar to her current life experiences e.g. solving a murder mystery. I particularly liked the murder mystery concept because although I had suspicions, I couldn't get tell who the "creature" was doing the killing.

Apart from the actual Addams Family, we are introduced to a whole cast of characters including Wednesday's Nevermore classmates, one of my favourites being Wednesday's roommate Enid Nightshade, a bubbly werewolf teen, the "Golden Retriever" to Wednesday's "Black Cat" personality. I love the way these two balance each other out. Throughout the series we see Wednesday being "not a hugger" and refusing Enid's advances of physical affection, until the last episode where they practically jump into each other's arms and never left go. That's what we call character development people!!!

The only thing I didn't enjoy about this TV show was the love triangle. Every teen show has one unfortunately and we could not get away from it, even with Wednesday. Despite her off-putting personality to other people, two boys begin fighting for her attention. We have Tyler, a "normie" barista that doesn't go to her school, and Xavier (whose name I had to Google because that's how memorable he was to me) her Nevermore classmate and also apparently a fellow psychic. I just felt like these love interests were bland and boring, Tyler slightly having the upper hand to be more interesting since he was involved more in the murder mystery plot but with Xavier, I genuinely didn't understand the appeal. He did nothing, and I definitely won't miss him in Season 2. Apparently the second season is going to be more of a "focus on horror" which I'm dying for!

I just don't think Wednesday would be interested in romance, despite her brief crush in *The Addams Family Values* and her relationship with Lucas in *The Addams Family Musical* which I mentioned in my Summerween section! There're actually a few call backs to the 90s films, with the *snap snap* from the theme song incorporated, Christina Ricci playing the teacher Miss Thornhill, and the theme of pilgrimage, as a reference to the weird Thanksgiving musical they performed in *Addams Family Values*. I'm glad they're choosing to bring more horror to the show, because Wednesday definitely does not have time for smooching when there's crimes to be solving!

The End.

Acknowledgements

Wow, I can't quite believe I'm writing the acknowledgments to my first ever book! When I first started planning and writing this book in 2022 & 2023, I knew it was going to be a big task. So much bigger than all of my half-written notebook attempts *ahem Chapter 1 by Megan Annie Scott*. But I believed in myself enough to start writing and stick with it. There's been many times where I abandoned the project altogether, left it on the back burner for months on end to then pick it up on a whim months later. But through all this time I stuck with it, and now here we are!

Now I didn't have a big publishing company backing me up, or a team of editors to help, just me, my laptop, and a big imagination. Which is exactly how my dad wrote his books, which is why I firstly want to thank my dad, Ken. Thank you for being the first author in the family, and showing that I could do it, I can do anything I can set my mind to, and also thank you for building my very own library. Even if I ran out of shelf-space...

Next I want to thank my Mam, Lynn possibly my biggest cheerleader. My Mam is also a bit like a witch herself. She knits and crochets and creates magic with her knitting needles. Not only is she a witch, but my safe place. She's always encouraged me with my dreams, even if I have boxes and boxes of half-filled notebooks and books in piles everywhere that probably drive her mad. Thank you for always coming along on my spooky adventures without hesitation and always telling me to believe in myself. I finally do.

I suppose I should thank my sisters next as we are technically Newcastle's answer to the *Sanderson Sisters*. Thank you to my oldest sister Kayleigh who I get a lot of my spooky interests from inherently. Your love of Halloween, Rocky Horror and creepy nail art has bled through into me (expect the nail art, I just like getting mine painted rather than being the artist) but I always admire your kooky vibe.

Thank you to my middle sister Lynsey. From you I love Stevie Nicks and skulls and will always be your favourite customer of *The Canny Haberdashery*. I admire how well you've created your small business, from being a hobby-hopper like me to creating something that people love and come back buying more. There's still plenty of space on my walls for more embroidery hoops! *Wink wink*

Thank you to a small human that has brightened up my life for nearly 3 years now. My niece, Orla. When I started writing this you were still a wee baby with your scrunched-up little face and cartoon blue eyes. Now you're a bouncy three-year-old with so much energy! When you were little, obviously you were still learning about the world, you still are! But now you understand so much more, especially about Halloween. Whenever I wear a spooky t-shirt, you love to have a good inspect or if I'm wearing one of my Halloween Loungefly backpacks you'll try and pick it up despite your soft toddler strength. And now even more excitedly, you actually like *Hocus Pocus*! If I'm wearing my crocs you'll exclaim "It's the funny witch!" and point to the Winifred Sanderson charm with delight. I really hope you love this book one day, when you learn how to read.

My thank yous now extend beyond the grave (sorry, bit morbid) to my grandparents. Firstly, to my Granda Richie. Ever since I was a child you told me I would be the next Catherine Cookson if I kept on writing. At the time I had no idea who Catherine Cookson was, but now I get it. One thing that saddens me, and hurts even as I'm writing this now, is that you will never get to read this book. I never got to show you any of my finished works before you passed away at the end of one of the shittiest years ever aka 2020. But that doesn't matter because you always believed in me anyway. I'm sending a ghost copy to wherever you are, so you can read it in spirit. I hope you like it.

Acknowledgements

Thank you to my grandma, Annie Means. We never got to meet unfortunately, as you died a couple of years before I was born. My Mam tells me all the time that looking at me is like looking at you, and I feel like that's a pretty big compliment. It wasn't until I started writing this book that I learned more about you. About how you believed in the paranormal, how you went to "spuggy" meetings and had a dalliance with a spirit or two. We are more alike than I realised. I feel honoured to feel closer to you than just a middle name, but an actual ghostly connection. I hope I've made you proud.

And finally, thank you to anyone who has written, directed, starred in a horror movie, designed a spooky t-shirt, piece of jewellery, a pin, sticker, or print, sang a scary song, written and published a horror/thriller novel, created a Halloween Instagram, and spread the love of Halloween across the internet and the world. If it wasn't for all of these people inspiring me, I never would have had the guts to change my bookish Instagram into a Halloween-themed account and became the witch I was always meant to be.

Yours terrifyingly, Apple-bobbing Annie x

Bibliography

Winterween

Winterween folk lore

- https://www.poetryfoundation.org/harriet-books/2016/12/the-mari-lwyd-dialogue-welsh-rhyme-battles-to-haunt-your-yuletide#:~:text=Mari%20Lwyd%2C%20Horse%20of%20Frost,They%20strain%20against%20the%20door.
- https://www.theguardian.com/lifeandstyle/2019/dec/18/the-seven-most-terrifying-christmas-traditions-around-the-world
- https://otherworldlyoracle.com/celebrate-krampusnacht/
- https://www.tripsavvy.com/krampus-parade-in-austria-tyrolean-christmas-festival-4154986
- https://www.standard.co.uk/news/world/when-krampusnacht-day-germany-tradition-christmas-b1041652.html

Ghostly Christmas traditions

- https://www.history.com/news/christmas-tradition-ghost-stories

Valloween

- The Rude, Cruel, and Insulting 'Vinegar Valentines' of the Victorian Era - Atlas Obscura
- Vinegar Valentines (and other spooky traditions)
- Scarlet Ravenswood (YouTube)
- All about Lupercalia
- Lupercalia: Meaning, Pagan Rituals, Valentine's Day - HISTORY
- Lupercalia festival meaning and rituals
- https://www.pastemagazine.com/movies/romance/best-monster-romances

Springoween (April)

Bibliography

National Bat Appreciation Day 2023: Things You Should Know (nationaldaystoday.com)

- Bat Appreciation Day (17th April)

The History of the Picnic | History Today

- National Picnic Day (23rd April)

Swedish Easter Traditions: Witches, Birch Twigs & Påskmust (scandinaviastandard.com)

- Wandering witches welcome Finnish Easter - thisisFINLAND
- Jackalopes of Wyoming – Myth or Reality? – Legends of America

Cemetery Appreciation month

- 12 Things You Need for a Cemetery Stroll - Spooky Little Halloween
- Victorian Funeral Customs and Superstitions – Friends of Oak Grove Cemetery
- Burke And Hare - The Sunderland Grave Robbers | Wearside Online
- 10 Victorian Cemetery Traditions - BillionGraves Blog
- Victorian Valhallas: Cemetery Picnics – The Midnight Society (midnightsocietytales.com)
- An introductory guide to Moscow graveyards - Russia Beyond (rbth.com)
- The Greeks Who Picnic on the Graves of Their Loved Ones (vice.com)
- Day of the Dead (Día de los Muertos) - Origins, Celebrations, Parade - HISTORY

Witch Trials

- The Witchcraft Act in Scotland | Historic Environment Scotland
- Women executed 300 years ago as witches in Scotland set to receive pardons | Scotland | The Guardian
- Scotland's Witch Prickers - The Real Mary King's Close (realmarykingsclose.com)

- Newcastle Witches | Newcastle Ghost Walks | Newcastle Witch History |
- Walpurgisnacht: The German Night of the Witches explained (iamexpat.de)

Bee Facts

- Learn these top 10 facts about bees | WWF
- Honey Bee Facts - 50 Things You Never Knew About Honey Bees! (buzzaboutbees.net)
- 10 Ways to Save the Bees - The Bee Conservancy

World Goth Day

- World Goth Day - May 22 - National Day Calendar
- 13 Of The Greatest And Most Famous Goth Rock Bands (hellomusictheory.com)
- www.sophielancasterfoundation.com
- Your Guide to Whitby Goth Weekend (yorkshirecoastalcottages.com)
- 125 Years of Dracula
- Record-breaking vampires at Whitby Abbey mark 125 years of Dracula | Bram Stoker | The Guardian
- Whitby Abbey - 125 Years of Dracula - England's Story - Collections (english-heritageshop.org.uk)
- Abbey illuminated with bats to mark 125 years of Dracula novel | Evening Standard

Plant Your Pumpkins

- How to grow pumpkins: all you need to know - The English Garden

Fairyween

- Fairy Witches: The Ages-old Connection Between Fae and Witchcraft (otherworldlyoracle.com)
- Ashley3 (girlguidingscotland.org.uk)

Summerween (June-July)

Pirate Ghosts

- https://www.grunge.com/248785/the-scariest-stories-of-pirate-ghosts/
- https://www.chroniclelive.co.uk/news/history/strange-tale-newcastles-very-real-life-8749439

The Story behind the Hoppings

- https://www.theguardian.com/uk/the-northerner/2012/jun/28/newcastle-thehoppings-fairground-rides-amuseuments

Are you a Sea Witch?

- https://www.moodymoons.com/2022/06/19/7-signs-youre-a-natural-sea-witch/

International Bat Night

- https://www.bats.org.uk/support-bats/international-bat-night

-History of Fish and Chips

- https://docksidehhi.com/the-history-of-fish-and-chips/#:~:text=Most%20people%20think%20that%20Fish,of%20necessity%2C%20not%20culinary%20genius.

Shaun of the Dead party ideas

- Shaun of the Dead Themed Party - Ideas and Inspiration (hotpartyshack.com)

<u>Autumnween (September-November)</u>

Berries of Autumn

- The Berries of Autumn - Marianne Willburn

Every Addams Family adaptation ranked

- The Addams Family' adaptations, ranked (ew.com)

Annie Fairlamb Mellon

- https://burialsandbeyond.com/2020/08/05/annie-fairlamb-mellon-the-geordie-medium/comment-page-1/

Ghost Hunting YouTube

- https://www.youtube.com/playlist?list=PLrwwpZzlar8_ohaKEfjlC6tRFmp-bSL1U
- https://www.youtube.com/results?search_query=glam+and+gore+ghost+hunt

History of Candy Corn

- https://www.bhg.com/halloween/recipes/the-history-of-candy-corn/#:~:text=Where%20Was%20Candy%20Corn%20Invented,turn%20of%20the%2020th%20century.

National Literacy Day

- https://nationaltoday.com/international-literacy-day/